KINGDOM OF ASH & BONES

CURSE OF THE DRAGONS
BOOK TWO

RAVEN STORM

Copyright © 2023 by Raven Storm

All rights reserved.

No part of this book may be reproduced in any form or by any electronic or mechanical means, including information storage and retrieval systems, without written permission from the author, except for the use of brief quotations in a book review.

Cover by Leigh Graphic Designs

❦ Created with Vellum

Also by Raven Storm

Kingdom of Flames & Flowers

Kingdom of Ash & Bones

Rise of the Drakens Series

The Lost Siren

The Lost Alliance

The Lost Kingdom

The Lost Nation

The Lost Princess

The Lost Child

The Lost King

The Lost Prince

Rise of the Alpha Series

Chained: Rise of the Alpha Book 1

Claimed: Rise of the Alpha Book 2

Changed: Rise of the Alpha Book 3

Box Set with Bonus Scenes

Aggie's Boys

The 40-Year-Old Virgin Witch

The Witch Who Couldn't Give Amuck

Hex Appeal

The Demon Chronicles (YA)

Descent

Feud

Royal Hunt

CHAPTER ONE

"Want to meet the demons?"

I'd just ditched out on my princes Zion and Zariah, and all my friends in the castle to get to the bottom of the dragon curse and what was going on with the Nobles. It had absolutely nothing to do with the fight Zariah and I had just had.

He'd said that's why your *people had been slaves. He'd said that.*

It hurt. It hurt so badly.

I left for my people, for the little girls in the mud district that were just like me, girls who were given an impossible choice of either marrying and breeding monsters, dying along the way, or falling victim to the discarded men who roamed the back allies. I'd suffered and scraped and clawed my entire life.

Or at least, that's what I was going to keep telling myself.

Pitch black and silent, the tunnel's air cloying. I

could feel the presence of my two friends next to me. There was another sound in the background that I couldn't make out yet. Whatever it was, it was loud and constant.

"You people always see the worst in everything! That's why you were slaves!"

Zariah's voice wouldn't leave my head.

I'd learned when I was four that words didn't matter; if you let them get to you, you'd be hungry and dead, or worse. Fireguards and mean men had called me every name in the book and it had never bothered me before.

You people.

That was the crux of the matter, wasn't it? The king had tried to warn me. No matter how elevated his station, he was still just a mud boy with no real power. My fate would be the same, wouldn't it? Even though mud blood ran through the prince's veins, they didn't grow up in the slums like the king and I had. They didn't understand.

In a way, I could understand the curse. People who gorged themselves on wine and food while others starved just down the mountain was enough to burn your veins and wish ruin upon every spoiled brat in the Seat.

That didn't mean anyone actually deserved to be cursed to turn into monsters, however.

You're running from your problems. You should stay and make them understand. You should stay for your mother. Heather and Hyacinthe need you. You're just abandoning them like you abandoned the mud quarter.

I bit my lip to chase away such morbid thoughts.

"Sorry for yelling," called out a familiar voice.

A small lit lantern illuminating Oleria, one of the girls I'd competed with but who had been too injured to continue, and Shava, my best friend from childhood who I never thought I'd see again.

"You set off one of the booby traps and then jumped me.... I wasn't ready." Oleria grinned crookedly, the twisted scars from the dragon's heat marring her once smooth face.

Shava rolled her eyes, but couldn't stop looking at me. I felt the same way; it had been years since we'd seen each other. What had she been up to? Did she know about the demons?

You wanted answers. Here they are.

I hadn't expected answers to literally fall into my lap courtesy of old friends who I'd thought dead or lost.

Zariah's words had left a gaping hole in my heart. Perhaps my friends could help fill in the chunks that had been torn out.

"Mari? Are you ok? Do you want to see a demon?" Oleria tilted her head at me, lips pursing with concern. I probably looked like a fright covered in dirt and muck from my descent down the balcony.

"Uh ... yes?" I squeaked out. I tamped down the worry that lingered in my gut about my mother, and tried to reassure myself that Ell would take care of her. He'd promised.

Oleria's scars from the dragon fire looked more defined and rigged where the small bit of light threw them into sharp relief. Shava looked older—that was to be expected. Her black hair was tied tightly back into a sleek ponytail, falling like an inky river down her back and fading into the utter darkness around us. Her eyes were just as they'd ever been—dark and haunted like mine, but with an underlying passion to care for everyone around her. There were small lines on her face that weren't there before her reaping, and she had a long, jagged scar on the left side of her neck.

Oleria reached out a wrapped hand to me, resting lightly on my shoulder. "I'm glad you made it out. I heard you won, though. Seems strange you've found your way here." She shot a glance at Shava. "The things we've heard and seen. There's much to catch up on. We can explain everything once we get there."

I nodded tightly, not trusting myself to speak lest hundreds of questions burst from my lips. It was surreal—my childhood friend and one of my palace friends, here together, leading me down into the depths of hell.

Maybe it was all a dream.

I tripped over an unseen root and fell hard on my face, cracking my nose. Pain exploded over me, quelling the dream theory. Shit.

"Careful. It's rough down here." Shava gave me her lantern and a rag from her pocket. I accepted both gratefully, holding the lantern low to the ground and pinching my nose with the rag to staunch the blood flow.

"Just follow, and we'll start talking," she said to me. As we made our way through the darkness, Shava spun her tale.

"I'm sure you've figured out quite a bit if you made it here, but I'll start at the beginning so nothing gets left out."

I nodded, then realized she couldn't see me since she was in front of me.

"Ok," I said, my voice echoing off the rock walls surrounding us.

We walked. The stone underneath us sloped down in increments as Shava said, "The year of the flux, they took everyone they could. I'm sure you remember. I was sick, but not badly enough so it didn't stop them from bringing me to the palace. I was bathed, dressed, and fed, but it felt like I was being prepped for something ... like a sacrifice, you know?"

I did know.

"There were so many girls that year. It was like they took everyone who wasn't sick. Girls as young as ten, the normal sixteen year olds, and they also took older mothers. The Fireguards ripped children from their mothers' arms and dragged them down the streets. You were sick and abed, so you missed it."

Shava paused. "Probably for the best. You must have been in really bad shape to be left alone."

I had been. I'd almost died.

Probably for the best.

"Anyway, there were fifty girls and women all together. They took care to bathe us in these giants bathtubs. They gave us fine clothes, and then ... and then ..." Shava's voice broke, and I feared what she would say next. Maybe she hadn't had to watch as girls drowned like I had, but what other horrible terrors had she seen?

"They fed us!" she finished dramatically, her voice hushed in the cave.

Oleria snorted, but I understood Shava instantly. At

least when Oleria and I had been taken, there'd been no qualms about this being a competition and that the Fireguards would happily weed out anyone not strong or smart enough to make it. But during Shava's year, they had been desperate for girls.

So they'd fed them in order to gain their trust.

"And then?" I asked, feeling as though it were the only appropriate thing to say. The stone floor around us leveled out as we kept going.

"They lined us up like the reaping, but this time the Nobles all came in and looked us over like we were pieces of meat fresh off the food wagon," she spat. "Every girl got picked by a Noble, and we were all wedded and bedded right there."

No one could see the horror stretched across my face in the darkness.

"Right ... there?!" I squeaked out, unable to imagine it. That many girls and that many Nobles ...

"You see, they knew what they were doing. They knew we'd freak out and fight, so it was more secure to keep us all in one big room—those bathing chambers, and just guard the doors. It was smart, actually," she added bitterly.

"Makes our time there sound a lot better. At least they pretended to treat us nicely," Oleria quipped.

"And you—" I cut myself off, unable to articulate the full thought. I couldn't verbalize the horror or even imagine it.

Shava huffed. "I did what I always do: use the chaos to my advantage. My Noble was older and blond. I let him lead me over to a corner. The Nobles all changed then—gray, flaking scaly skin underneath their fancy tunics, with hands cold as ice. They were the walking dead and needed us to make fresh, alive babies. The Nobles are all dying. They're part of this curse just as much as the dragon overhead."

I held my tongue on that. It wasn't time yet. "The Nobles are all ... what? These demon creatures?" I asked instead, wondering if they knew more than I did. It was one thing to think about it, and quite another to hear it confirmed. I thought of the snarling monsters Zariah and I had uncovered in the caves. It was all connected, wasn't it? Zariah and Zion—the princes—were under a separate curse from the Nobles. Their dragon forms could attest to that.

"The Nobles are cursed as well. They're all turning into demons," I amended quickly.

Shava paused ahead of me along with Oleria, our torches throwing heavy shadows under our faces.

"That's why they want the uncursed girls from the other quarters. That's especially why they want mud girls, and why the queen has a mud boy for her king," Shava declared.

My brow furrowed. "They can't have demon children; that would hardly go unnoticed unless they can't have children at all. They're using the uncursed girls to—"

"Try and lessen the curse with each next generation, hoping that eventually they weaken it to the point where they can stop changing and beat the curse."

Nausea swirled in my stomach as Hyacinth's desperate pleas from the closet rang in my ears. *"Can't have babies. Cursed. That's why they need us. That's why all their girls are primas. Help me get away. We need to get away!"*

I swallowed back the bile that threatened to come up my throat. "Is it ... working?" I asked, almost afraid to hear the answer.

Oleria laughed, a bit hysterically. Shava's head shook back and forth. "Come and see." She grabbed my hand and pulled me through the darkness. My thoughts kept going back to what she'd said about her reaping ... wedding and bedding.

"Shava, I'm sorry, but what happened—"

"I killed my husband, that's what happened," she snapped back, not bothering to look back at me. "Before his cold, dead hands could put his cold, dead dick inside of me I ripped it off like the rotten bit of sausage it was. There was so much screaming and crying and running that the Fireguards had their hands full. Remember the large windows in the bathing house?"

Not really, but I'd been understandably focused on other things at the time. Such as the murdering and the drowning. But I remembered how airy and bright the bathhouses were—that meant there had to have been large windows.

"I dove straight out. Didn't even look at what was below. Figured even death was better than whatever that was. I got lucky; I landed on a passing Fireguard who promised not to tell anyone I'd escaped and actually led me to the same passage you found. I followed it and found the others."

A sympathetic Fireguard? There was no such thing. Unless ... that didn't make any sense. They were my age, weren't they? A Fireguard had to be a man, not a teenager. Shava had been reaped five years before me. None of the numbers made sense. Had it been Ell?

"The others?" I asked instead, wanting desperately for something I could wrap my brain around.

Shava grinned, but it lacked any true mirth. "You'll see."

A roaring sound reached us from up ahead, growing louder as we approached. It couldn't be a dragon, could it? No, that was all wrong. Shava held my hand so tightly I was unable to pull away.

Dim torches caught my eye as we came out in a narrow hallway lined with stone. The roaring sound was below me and to the sides, and as my eyes adjusted to the dim lighting, a narrower stone walkway stretched out before us.

"Be careful!" Oleria yelled over the roar. "If the current gets you, it'll whip you to the next kingdom before you blink!"

Current? Next kingdom?

"Watch your step!" Shava yelled back as the path narrowed, pointing down. The gleam off the wet stones was the only thing I could see—and I realized it was from water. The stones were wet and slick because an entire goddamn river rushed on either side of us. The sound was deafening.

I clutched Shava's hand, terrified. After the bathhouse when I'd almost drowned, I hated water and everything to do with it. Shava patted my hand once, then pulled me after her without an ounce of sympathy. Oleria followed behind as she extinguished our torches and forced us to rely on the small ones dotting the stone walls on either side of us.

A large iron gate ahead seemed to be our destination. What was only a few hundred paces felt like miles. Too scared to properly pick my feet up, I did an awkward shuffle to make sure I always had contact with the slick rocks underneath me. Shava gripped me tightly, but didn't complain about my pace. Neither did Oleria behind me.

I was afraid of falling and dying, but I was more afraid of never finding answers.

I kept moving.

Once I was close enough, I fell at the foot of the iron gate, wrapping my hands and fingers around the cold, wet iron as if I could anchor myself there forever.

"Mari, gonna have to let go or they can't let us in," Shava chortled. Oleria pulled me back as the iron gate rose up, disappearing into a crack in the stone above us.

"Let's go."

The moment Oleria cleared the gate behind me, it slammed back down so hard my ears rung and the breeze lifted the edges of my hair.

"Can't be too careful. If the queen finds out, she'd torch the place."

I let the comment slide. I could absolutely see her using Zariah or Zion (even both) to turn all of her enemies to ash. Again.

Beyond the gate lay darkness. Our footsteps echoed around the stone walls and floor, and opened up into an underground cavern that was narrow but with a much calmer stream of water running down two sides.

"Over the years, they managed to divert and dam a good portion of it to make it safe and usable for everyone here," Shava lectured. Rows of tents and makeshift forts made of scrap fabric and blankets lined the path ahead of us. Bits of tied string nailed or shoved into crevices and cracks in the stone walls and mortar held up the fabric. My home in the mud quarter had been nothing to brag about, but it hadn't been this bad.

Bodies lay inside of the tents, most of them with feet sticking out of the ends. Pale, grey skin met my eyes. Some figures huddled outside the tents with little fires, trying desperately to shake off the chill that hung in the moist air. No one would meet my gaze. The air was filled with the moans and groans of dozens of people.

"All demons were once Nobles, and all Nobles become demons?" I asked quietly, trying to imagine it.

"Yes. Come here." Shava kneeled down next to the third tent, made out of a tunic that might have been blue at one point. The figure inside groaned when we approached, but didn't move.

"You see?" Shava asked, pointing at the exposed, ashy gray skin on his legs. "Not much is known about when the curse first came, but like I said, we do know they're trying to combat it by diluting their blood lines as much as possible. It's met with limited success. The children still end up turning, but not until the hit their majority."

I studied the man's face—sickness aged him, but his face was young and free of any lines and wrinkles. How old was he, then?

"So what? They are sent down here when the change gets too much?" I asked, thinking of poor Heather and Hyacinth. And Azalea. And Leilani. And, I supposed, Freesia. No one won in this scenario.

I bent down next to the man, unable to just leave

him suffering. Shava huffed in annoyance, crossing her arms over her chest. I ignored her and brushed the man's hair out of his face. His eyes fluttered open.

"The princess ..." he breathed out.

A dark chuckle rumbled in my chest. "I'm no princess."

His hand twitched and tried to rise, seeking mine. I met him halfway, entwining my fingers with his cold, brittle ones.

"But you are the dragon rider. The one who will make it all stop ..."

Every fear and insecurity rose up within me, but the man looked so happy, so finally at peace with the world, that I couldn't say anything to take it from him.

So I sucked it up, and gave a big, fake smile. "Yes. I will."

He gave my hand one last squeeze, his smile radiant as his eyes closed. His hand went limp against mine as his expression smoothed out into sleep.

"Coming?" Shava asked pointedly.

I stood reluctantly and joined the other two. "Do all the changing Nobles come here?"

Oleria bit out a dark laugh. "The smart ones find their way down here. They figure out what's happening and leave before the queen gets them. It's better than the alternative." She shot a dark look to Shava, whose brows furrowed.

"And that is?" I pointedly asked.

Shava leaned in. "I heard rumors the dragon was heard in the west mines a week ago. Would you know anything about that?" Shava asked coolly, her voice tinged with accusation.

My back stiffened in defense. "What of it?"

"You risk the entire kingdom's destruction, that's what," called a familiar voice. I spun around so fast I nearly slipped on the wet stone, my heart thudding in my chest. He was so achingly familiar looking, and yet not. Confusion stopped my breath in its tracks.

CHAPTER
TWO

Breathe.

B He could have been Zion or Zariah, yet wasn't. He was older, for one thing. Not by much, but I could tell in how he carried himself with authority and experience. His face was more serious, with a square jaw and a heavier brow that made him heavily favor the king, and his eyes weren't silver with green—they were just like mine. He wore boots with leather pants and a tunic that looked like it had seen better days. The hem of his pants and his sleeves were a hodgepodge of materials, as if he'd quickly outgrown it and needed to keep adding to it.

It was still much finer than anything I'd ever worn in the mud quarter.

"I—"

"Zephyr. Don't look too shocked." He held out his hand, smiling with just enough confidence mixed with bashfulness that it was charming. Something Zion and Zariah distinctly lacked.

I closed my mouth, gritting my teeth so hard it hurt. "Who—"

"The bastard prince. Well, really that's just my name for it. It sounds a lot better than 'the experiment,' don't you think?"

My mouth dropped open while Shava gave me a little push in my back, giving Zephyr big, doe eyes. "Let's go to your tent for a bit of privacy?"

Zephyr rolled his eyes. "Like this lot cares or will be sane enough to pass along anything they overhear." Still, he led the way down the rows of tents, the small little homes becoming more spacious and elaborate the further into the tunnels we went. The people who sat outside fires and lounged about didn't look sick or sad here—simply tired. They gave Zephyr little half-smiles and waves, bent over sewing or cooking. Nearly all of them were women, ranging from just older than me to elderly women with gray hair! I kept my mouth shut though, determined to save all my questions until I could sit down.

We paused before a massive stone door, which was as large as the cave opening itself. Zephyr gestured to the last tent on the left, the closest to it. He held open the flap for Oleria and Shava, but I couldn't stop staring at the gigantic slab of stone. It was one giant piece from floor to ceiling, carved with intricate swirls and designs in a grandiose work of art.

Zephyr cleared his throat, giving me a pointed look. Right.

I ducked inside with the others, looking around with curiosity. His tent was a hodgepodge of many things—rather like his clothing. The tent itself was haphazardly sewn together out of what he could find, but it was quite large which made it roomy inside. The fabric was stretched and pinned upwards, toward a small hole in the middle to let out smoke from the small fire pit. Around the fire were two large logs propped up with stones. The back section of the tent was sectioned off with more fabric, and I suspected his private sleeping area was hidden away behind it. Off to the right in the corner was a collection of crates and boxes.

"Sit, please. Would you like something to eat or drink?"

Oleria and Shava sat down around his fire with a familiarity that made me realize just how quickly the world had turned on me. I stared in wonder as Zephyr headed over to the boxes and crates, quickly pulling out a few chipped clay plates as well as some meat and a large pan.

"It'll be just a minute."

He put the pan over the fire and tossed the meat in, setting the plates down on the log. He disappeared behind the flap in the back, and returned with three cups of sweet-smelling juice. Oleria and Shava took their offered cups gratefully, but I hesitated.

"Is it wine?" I asked, not unreasonably.

He laughed. "No, none of that down here. We need to keep our wits about us."

I took the cup as Shava grimaced and Oleria sighed. It smelled fruity, but not at all sharp and bitter like the wines the Fireguards gave out in the mud quarter. Tentatively, I took a sip.

My eyebrows went to my forehead. It was so sweet! And ... good!

The sizzling sound of meat brought my attention to

the fire, along with the fresh aromas that went along with it.

"Are you going to sit down?" Zephyr eyed me with one dark eyebrow raised while he crouched next to the fire, patiently flipping over the meat when needed and sprinkling some spices from a pouch at his waist. I felt so detached from reality it was hard to respond. There was a man cooking for me ... and serving me. And his expressions were so like Zion and Zariah's, it caused a physical ache in my chest.

"Mari, don't be rude. Sit down." Shava grabbed my wrist and yanked me down on the log next to her. I almost spilled my cup but recovered, not wanting to waste one precious drop.

"Are you related to the princes?" I blurt out, the only thought running through my mind.

"Sorry about her, she's from the same place I am," Shava offered, rolling her eyes skyward. I shot her a glare.

Zephyr just chuckled. "It's all right. At least you already know there are two of them and their true nature. That will make this much easier." He paused, flipping the meat once more. Juices crackled and spat out from the side of the pan, hot and delectable. I wasn't sure what I wanted more at that moment: food or answers.

Why not both?

"But to answer your *burning* question, yes. I am related. Though I was never acknowledged as being their half-brother. Otherwise I wouldn't be here."

The last part was said lightly, but with a bit of an edge to it. I blushed. It was probably a sore subject for him, and here I was prodding the open wound. I took another sip of my precious juice to mull it over. "Half-brother," I muttered out loud. From which side? The queen?

No, it was obvious from the heaviness of his face. He was the king's son through and through. But did that mean—

"Before your brain explodes, why don't you eat and I'll explain? I'm not particularly hungry at the moment, and I rarely get much of a chance to entertain new people."

Zephyr grabbed the plates and carefully doled out pieces of meat to each of us, leaving nothing for himself. "I had a loaf of bread, but I gave it to Elenor earlier today. Her kids wanted it."

His face flushed as though not being able to offer bread with our meat was a horrible transgression.

I barely grasped the rough edges of the plate before I picked up the meat with my bare hands and tore into it, unprepared for how hot it was. I dropped it automatically, wincing.

"Sorry. Not used to hot food. You remember how I was," Shava offered to Zephyr.

My eyes narrowed at her. I was getting real sick of her apologizing on my behalf like there was something wrong with me.

Luckily, the meat had only fallen to my plate, though it wouldn't have mattered to me. I'd eat it covered in dirt if I had to; I'd certainly done worse when hungry. Though Shava would likely yell at me. Since when did she have such developed manners anyway?

Zephyr frowned at me. "Weren't you living at the palace?"

"For all of two weeks," I muttered back, touching the meat with the tip of my finger to gauge the heat. Feeling it had cooled considerably, I took a neat little bite, and moaned out loud at the taste. It wasn't as fancy on my tongue as the palace food, but that only made it better—just a bit of salt and some other spice, and juicy as can be. All of my attention focused on the meat and I gulped it down before realizing what I did.

I burped.

Shava opened her mouth.

"You better not be about to apologize for me," I warned her, wiping my mouth with the back of my hand. Her lips snapped shut as Oleria chuckled.

"Told you she was a handful," she remarked playfully.

"This is fun and all, but some answers would be nice," I grit out.

Zephyr smiled patiently, and sat back on his log across from us. "Answers. Wouldn't we all like answers? I suppose it would be easiest to start with myself?"

I gestured around to the cave. "And this place. And how these Nobles got here, what's going to happen to them, and all about the people here who don't seem to be sick."

Shava huffed. "So everything."

Oleria gave her a playful shove. "Shut it."

Zephyr gave them a tolerant look, then focused his attention on me. Seeing my mother's eyes, Shava's eyes, my eyes, looking back at me from his face made me feel a host of emotions: hope, fear, anxiety, and longing.

"You're the king's son," I started with, feeling pretty sure about that one.

"Son is a bit of a generous term," he began with not a small trace of bitterness in his voice. "It was an experiment to see how deep the curse went through the generations of Nobles, and whether or not a cure was in sight."

I let that settle in my mind. "So ... the king had you on purpose?" I snorted. "I bet the queen loved that."

Zephyr leveled me with a cool stare. "I'm told it was her idea. She wanted insurance that breeding with a mud boy would give her heirs that wouldn't share the Nobles' curse and try to eat the staff."

I think that was his attempt at a joke, but it fell flat with the amount of dying Nobles spread around us.

"The queen picked a Noble woman who had mud quarter descent as well as artisan quarter descent, and she was only a Noble for a generation and a half. The result was ... me. And that gave the queen the confidence to have her sons. Though, I bet no one could have foreseen the curse they'd be under was so different."

"So you know they're twins, and you know they're the dragon. Dragons," I corrected, a headache blossoming at my temples.

"I've learned a lot over the years, being cast out and having to make my own way," he answered, which wasn't really much of an answer.

I raised an eyebrow, a silent question. There was a lot about him that was eerily similar to me.

He sighed. "I was allowed to be raised by my mother in the Noble court until I was five and the queen gave birth to the prince. Or princes. I didn't find that out until much later. Even so, I was torn from my mother's arms and sent to the Seat to train. The queen didn't want any competition hanging around her precious little princes."

"Oh, so just like every other boy from the mud quarter," I quipped, not feeling too bad for him. At least he'd been able to live in the luxury of the Seat for his first five years, and not the squalor and hunger my brother and I had to deal with.

Thinking of my brother made me slightly ill, so I shook my head and moved on.

"Well, obviously you aren't a Fireguard," I pointed out.

Zephyr's face darkened. "I did too well. I called attention to myself. The queen didn't like how heavily I favored the king and her princes. So she ordered me killed a few years ago, right before I completed my Fireguard training."

I couldn't help the laugh that burst from my mouth. Oleria covered her mouth in shock, and Shava frowned. "Sorry," I gasped, waving my hands around. "But it's just ... we should form a club. 'I survived the queen trying to kill me' or something ridiculous like that."

Zephyr looked a tad offended. "Well, she tried to kill me by pushing me off the wall."

I grinned. "She tried feeding me to Zariah."

Zephyr blinked. "Is that how you tamed the dragon? You were ... with the prince? Or both? Fascinating ..."

The urge to defend what small scraps of honor I had left rose within me. "For your information, I didn't give myself to him. Well not then. That came after. I mean—" I slammed my mouth shut blushing furiously. "So she pushed you off the wall and you lived?" I pushed on desperately, anxious to move on.

"Well, that's how I found out the dragon was actually the prince. He caught me on his back and spirited me away. I'd never seen the queen so angry before. He dropped me in front of a tunnel and told me it was the best he could do and to disappear. He said he was sorry he couldn't know me better, and wished me luck."

I blinked. "So, was it Zion or Zariah?"

Zephyr shrugged his shoulders. "He didn't say, and I don't know either of them well enough to venture a guess."

Hmm. It seemed like the sort of thing Zion would want to do, but then again, Zariah was the one who actually had the balls to disobey his mother as much as he could and help others.

Which also meant Zion and Zariah knew about Zephyr this entire time and didn't mention it to me once. My gut twisted just a little bit more.

"Anyhow, I dove into the tunnels and found this entire system that connects to the old mines and goes under most of the kingdom. It was a bit touch and go at first, but I learned how to steal food from the castle and other things I needed to survive." Zephyr's expression darkened. "Then about a year later, the Nobles started showing up in my tunnels. All starting from the same one the prince dropped me off at, the same one you came from."

Shava took over, shooting a concerned glance at Zephyr. "We suspect the prince—one of them, or both—is trying to save the dying Nobles for a reason. Zephyr figured out the warning signs when a change is imminent, so we have a pretty accurate timeline of how long someone has before they'll shift."

"And then what?" I asked with horrified fascination. "You kill them?"

Oleria huffed, and Shava's face pinched. "Well, no. Zephyr doesn't think we should kill them. He thinks the princes want us to save them—otherwise why not just let the queen murder them as she has been?"

"The queen kills her own subjects?" I clarified, though it wasn't hard for me to imagine.

"The queen makes the dragon kill them. Shoves them all up on top of the dome and roasts them down to ashes. It's the only thing I know of that definitively kills them," Zephyr said sadly.

Oh, no. Poor Zion. Poor Zariah.

"So, to honor the prince saving my life, I honor this unspoken request. I let them shift here in the safety of the stone tunnels, which are blocked off and can't be accessed unless you know how to open the massive doors, which no one does other than myself." He paused, grinning wryly. "I am a prince in a way, just like them: the bastard prince of the demons!"

Kinship with this mysterious bastard prince surged through me. He was just trying to look out for the condemned Nobles, just like I'd been trying to look out for the people of the mud quarter. Zephyr was more like me than Zion or Zariah ever would be!

That's your anger talking, my inner voice chastised. I ignored it, forcing myself back to the conversation at hand.

The way he looked at Shava had me putting a few pieces together in my head. That and the way she blushed like mad, refusing to meet his eyes. Shava was never bashful.

His gaze turned to me, angry. "Which is why you endangered the entire kingdom when you opened the mineshaft last week. Thank the gods, the dragon closed it behind him, otherwise the terror and destruction that would have been unleashed would have been unimaginable."

I held up a hand. "So you're telling me you just let all the Nobles shift into ... those demon things we saw?"

That didn't seem safe or responsible.

"Well, not all the Nobles. It's complicated. Wives are taken from the other quarter, so they aren't cursed. Any daughters born to those unions are still cursed, but it's diluted. It makes them unfit to be mothers, so they become primas. The ones that escape are allowed to live here. We shove the demons down into the mines when they shift. We can't endanger the others who live here, after all."

My mouth gaped open. That seemed ... I didn't know which was worse: putting them out of their misery or assigning them to a cursed life underground. And only the males? Well, that ... made sense. I remembered the large number of girls who had prepared with my friends and I, ready to be given over as the next crop of primas.

"So ... where are the Noble women who were cursed?" I asked, unable to get past this gaping hole in his story. The fire pop and cracked, and I jumped. I wasn't used to seeing any fire, letting alone the hisses and noises of the one right in front of me.

Zephyr frowned, picking up a long stick and prodding ashes in the pit to the side. He went to a small pile of wood and hefted a larger piece, throwing it onto the fire with a grunt. I jumped as sparks spit and fanned out from the fire, and pinned me with a look. "What do you think the queen would do with them?"

Oh, the demons. Right. Nothing good.

The smell of wood and ash filled the tiny tent, and Shava spoke up, continuing to stare into the growing flames. "We check about once a week for new people. The princes can't save too many of them because of course the queen would be suspicious if she ran out of demon-Nobles to scorch."

Which meant Zion and Zariah had to pick and choose who would live and who would die.

My hungry existence in the mud district suddenly didn't seem quite as bad in comparison. I eyed this new 'prince' in a new light; he was a young man without any of the queen's blood in him, a young man who deeply cared about helping those less fortunate than him.

Careful, flower.

I ignored the warning voices in my head. It wasn't like that. You could admire someone without falling in love with them, and it was clear he belonged to Shava, anyway.

It was just nice to find someone with common goals and interests, someone who hadn't grown up with a full belly and understood what it meant to suffer and starve.

Zephyr might be the key to all of this.

CHAPTER
THREE

It was a lot to take in, but to Zephyr's credit, he kept going as long as I had questions. That was more than Zion and Zariah had given me.

"Since you grew up in the Seat, did you ever learn about the curse or how all this started?" I asked, unable to help myself.

Shava rolled her eyes, as if already bored by the conversation. The way she hung onto Zephyr was annoying. How did he stand it?

He gave her an indulgent pat on her arm, and faced me. "I know a fair bit. It's all there in the archives, but not in any language we speak."

Oh. That at least made me feel a little better. Even if I could read, I wouldn't have been able to figure it out anyway.

It was his smug grin that made my eyes roll next. "I'm guessing you can, though?" I prompted.

He reminded me of Freesia in a way, desperate to lord his knowledge over others. I had no problem playing into that to learn what I needed to know, just like I'd done with her.

Zephyr leaned in as though what he was about to say was a secret despite only Shava and Oleria sitting near us. "I taught myself how to read the slave language. Painstakingly, I developed a cipher to figure out common letters and pieced together most of it from there. It took me three years!"

I shot a look at Shava as he casually mentioned the 'slave language,' but she was all doe eyes for her bastard prince.

"The slave language?" I repeated.

Zephyr blinked as if he realized who he was talking to.

"Well ... sorry. That was insensitive, wasn't it? There are records dating back to when Barcenea started importing people: your people. Along with those records, a bunch started appearing in this new language. It only made sense that it was the native language. They must have employed one of them as a scribe at one point, but the writings ceased after twenty years or so, probably at the scribe's death."

My people? He looked more like a mud boy than I did a mud girl. He didn't need to say the next part since it was implied. With the death of the people who'd known to read their own language, it was lost. And then eventually, we lost the spoken bits entirely. How long had it taken? One generation? Two?

"How old were these texts?" I asked, a bit numb.

He rubbed his jaw with his thumb, happy to have an audience. "Hard to say. Hundreds of years for sure."

"So ... the people worked in the mines," I grumbled. "And then?"

Zephyr continued with enthusiasm. "It's fascinating, really. The slave texts told all kinds of fantastical stories, including ones about guardian dragons who would watch over them all." He snorted. "Ridiculous, right?"

I wanted to punch him in his smug little face. How could he be so ignorant? Half of the blood that ran through his veins was the same mud blood as Shava's and mine! Yet he spoke so disparagingly of his own heritage and culture—our heritage and culture! But one word stuck out to me, and forced me to rein my temper in.

"Dragons? That doesn't seem like a coincidence."

I chanced a glance at Oleria, who was listening with rapt attention, eyes wide.

Zephyr laughed, waving a hand dismissively. "If you could read it, you would understand. It was fantastical tales of dragons as some kind of guardians ... and witches of all things! Can you imagine? This doddering fool scribbled on and on about witches and their magicks, and how they could cast curses—"

"Curses?!" I squawked out, unable to help myself.

Zephyr raised an eyebrow sarcastically. "Many magicks are unknown." His hand waved haphazardly again, and the flames in the fire flickered. My eyes narrowed at him. Something was off about his demeanor, but it wasn't like I knew him well enough to say for sure.

"Just like dragons are unknown?" I countered, glaring at him.

Shava eyed both of us. "I think that's enough for one night. Maybe you'd like to get settled into your own tent, and we can come back in the morning?"

Shava asked me, but her concerned gaze was still on Zephyr, who'd gone silent and stared moodily into the fire.

"All right," I conceded, still in a bit of a daze from everything I'd learned. Oleria lifted her burned, wrapped hand to mine, and quietly led me out of the tent. Shava stood abruptly, shoving something at me.

"Here, take this. Everyone down in the tunnels carries flint and some materials for a torch. Light is survival, down here. Keep them tied to you at all times. They're more important than a sword."

She handed me a large sack and a small one. I accepted the materials, staring down at them in confusion.

"Oh, that's right. They don't teach us how to make fire in the mud quarter, do they?" Shava gave me a lopsided grin, her eyes a bit sad. My earlier frustration with her slid away. It wasn't her fault we drifted away from each other. It wasn't her fault we were struggling to do the best we could.

"Yeah, well, I don't think even the Flames know how," I joked back.

Her eyes sparked for a moment with her old joy, and she sat me down and dumped out the small little satchel she'd given me onto the stones. One by one, she pointed at the strange objects littering the ground, starting with a curious metal hook.

"This is your striker. You use it with your flint." She indicated a flat bit of rock, holding them up together with one in each hand. "To build a flame, you take a small piece of this charcoal—" She picked up a thin shaving of black rock, and folded it over the small rock (or flint, as she called it). Taking the hook (striker, she said), she hit it against the rock and charcoal over and over again, creating vibrant red sparks.

My eyes widened with interest. After about the tenth strike, a small glow emanated from the charcoal shaving. I bent down close over it, both our heads nearly touching.

"You see? Now we have an ember."

Shava picked up a small bundle of dried grass and put the charcoal piece deep inside, then blew ever so gently on it.

My jaw dropped as the entire thing burst into flames.

"Now quickly, open your large bag and pull out the torch."

Not wanting to mess it up, I fumbled a bit at untying the strings before I pulled out a long torch made from a log, the top wrapped in cloth. Shava used one hand to unravel the cloth, revealing a sticky tar underneath.

"I won't do it now and waste your torch, but then you simply add this flame to the torch, and there you have it!"

She blew out the flames in her hand, letting the burned remains drop to the ground. "Oh, I guess I used your materials. Here, switch with me, and I'll get more in the morning."

She dug out her own satchel and replaced my dried grass with hers, grinning widely. I was still a bit in shock at this new, very important skill she'd so freely taught me. For just a split second, it felt like old times. Shava was teaching me, and protecting me.

A few tents down, a sick Noble coughed, shattering the illusion. I glanced back up. Zephyr had disappeared, no doubt to the back of his tent behind the privacy curtain.

"Did Zephyr teach you this?" That was the only thing I could come up with.

Her smile turned wistful and dreamy. "Yeah. He's great, right? So smart. He knows how to do everything."

It was on the tip of my tongue to argue it was because we'd been stuck in the mud quarter most of our lives and he was brought up in the Seat, but I choked it back. Shava and I were both very different people than we were as girls. I had to at least try.

"That's ... great. I better get to sleep," I said rather dully.

Shava gave me a wave and a quick hug. Oleria offered to show me to my tent, which I accepted. Outside and away from the mysterious bastard prince, I was able to focus on my more recent friend. "Did the prince save you as well?"

Her burned face twisted with a grimace, which was her new smile. "Yes. Wisteria is around here somewhere. He tries to save as many girls as he can. Said it's a meager penance, but it's the only thing that lets him sleep at night."

Oleria guided me down three tents, stopping at an empty one. "I'm right next to you on the right."

"And Shava?" I asked.

Oleria's scarred face twitched. "She bunks with Zephyr."

Of course she did.

"Thanks." Exhaustion settled into my bones.

Oleria turned to move away, but something in me

didn't want her to go. "Wait," I said suddenly, reaching out with one hand.

She turned, an expectant look in her eyes.

"Can we just ... how have you been?" I asked desperately. "None of us saw you after your injury, and we assumed the worst. Now you're here, and ..." I trailed off, not sure what else to say.

Her lips thinned in a ghost of what might have been a grin weeks ago, but now was only twisted flesh. She gestured to a log outside of my tent and we both sat down.

Silence descended between us.

"I'm ... sorry we didn't check on you. After the ..." I gestured vaguely at my face, then blushed when I realized how inconsiderate I was being.

Oleria tucked a piece of hair behind her ear, exposing her scarred face all the more. At least she wasn't self-conscious about it. "I would have liked to see you try," she chuckled darkly. "You remember where we had our ... examination?"

An unconscious shiver went down my spine. I tried not to, but it was branded in my memory forever. Seeing that look in my eyes, Oleria's eyes darted to the floor.

"Well, they kept me down there to 'recover.' I don't really think they wanted me to get better, though. It seemed like I was a giant inconvenience."

I snorted. "Wouldn't go quietly into that great beyond, eh?"

Her brow furrowed. "You think that was it? They were hoping I'd just die?"

My shoulders shrugged. "Did they feed you? Wrap your wounds? Give you a goddamn poultice?"

Oleria winced. "No. I ... fuck."

My eyes widened as the expletive tumbled from her lips. I was used to being the only girl who swore, which was unlike these gently bred ladies from the other quarters.

"What is it?" I asked.

Her eyes closed halfway, deep in thought. "I'd figured they had been the ones to wrap my wounds, you know? It happened days and days after they'd first brought me back to the room and left me there, but you're right; that doesn't make sense. I ... I think ..." She frowned.

I was impatient to press her further, but held it in. She'd get there on her own time.

"I think Zephyr did it. He was the one who carried me here and saved me. I never realized he bandaged me as well, but it makes sense, doesn't it?"

Yeah, it did. He likely had some basic medical training from his studies in the Seat.

"What do you remember about it?" I asked.

She sighed. "Pain that didn't abate until someone put a poultice on my hands and face and wrapped it. I remember dark hair bent over me and being carried. Then nothing until I woke up here."

I frowned. It sounded like Zephyr.

"Well, however it happened, I'm glad it got done. I'm happy to see you made it."

Oleria beamed up at me, and I decided the fire hadn't disfigured her at all. She was just as beautiful as she'd always been—perhaps, even more so, because now we were free.

"I'm so happy you're here, Mari. We need someone

like you around." She stood and gave me another hug before straightening and pulling away.

"Thanks," I managed bashfully.

Oleria nodded. "No problem. I'm going to check on some things, then I'll be right back. Let me know if you need anything at all."

I ducked inside my tent as she disappeared down the row. There was already a small cot inside with a thin folded blanket on top. The tent fabric itself was thin, but it was clean. And it was mine.

I sat down carefully on the cot's edge. It beat the dirt floor in my mother's hut any day. Unfolding the blanket with a snap of my wrist, carefully I stretched out on my back. My eyes drifted shut immediately. This would be good for me, right? I could continue to explore the secrets of the tunnels, the demons, and the curse with Zephyr's knowledge, and then I could work with him to help Zion and Zariah. I would go back for the other girls when I could. I—

A piercing scream cut through the air: high-pitched and terrified. Adrenaline pumped through my veins as I jumped straight up from the cot, nearly falling on my face as I tripped over it in my hurry to get outside the tent. I ran down the row in the same direction Oleria had gone; curious heads stuck out from nearby tents as I raced by.

"What's going on? Is it code black?" one young woman yelled at me, her young son clutching tightly to her skirts.

"Maybe!" I yelled back over my shoulder, figuring it was a safe answer since I had no idea what the hell she was talking about. Watching as she and the others around her exploded into action, it seemed to be the right call. Either way, I ran toward the screaming, which sounded just in front of me before it cut off abruptly in the middle of the cluster of sick Nobles' tents.

I skidded to a stop in front of a tent that had been torn down and ripped to shreds. A demon creature snarled at me, completely ashen with black scales and red eyes. A gold necklace around its neck winked at me, scraps of a fine tunic clinging to its frame. The creature spat and hissed, fangs dripping with blood. At its feet lay what was left of Oleria.

Out of all the terrible things I'd seen and witnessed in my life, this was the worst, bringing my entire mind and body to a screeching halt.

I screamed.

And screamed, and screamed.

All around me sick Nobles stumbled and crawled, trying to put as much distance between themselves as the demon as possible. This would be their fate too, but not yet.

More screams erupted from further down the row as the word spread that a Noble had turned too early. Pounding footsteps headed toward me, and a heavy hand landed on my shoulder, pushing me back.

Shava.

She had a long whip in her hand and a look of vengeance in her eyes. Zephyr was right behind her, swinging an extensive length of chain around his wrist. The cowering Nobles flinched away from them as though they were death personified.

Which I guess they were, in a way.

They didn't pause in horror or startle at the sight of Oleria's mangled corpse. Single-mindedly focused, they moved in on the demon. Shava cracked her whip over its chest, sending it stumbling to the ground and roaring in pain. The moment it fell, Zephyr moved in, wrapping it in chains while Shava kept its fangs and claws in check with her whip.

In short order, the creature was trussed up before me, dark blood bleeding out onto the stones.

"Fuck, he had three days left," Shava panted, shooting a frightened glance at Zephyr, who frowned deeply.

"He must have lied about when his symptoms started then," he shot back in a way that implied the subject was closed.

Shava's jaw dropped. "They can't all be lying about—"

"Get rid of the body. The kids shouldn't see it."

Zephyr turned on his heel and yanked the demon after him like it was a particularly disobedient dog.

A dog that had just torn my friend apart.

"Mari, step away. Come with me to send this demon where it belongs," Zephyr ordered.

I stepped away from Shava and Oleria automatically, but only because I didn't want to throw up what precious food I'd just eaten by staying any longer. I couldn't separate the snarling creature in front of me from the sick Noble he'd likely just been. It was strange to see the shift in Zephyr. Hadn't he just been going on about saving everyone he could? Now he eyed the demon like an insect that was about to be squashed under his foot.

"Stupid, bloody—"

"You didn't expect him to change so quickly?" I asked and I thought Zephyr ignored me as he grunted and pulled. I grabbed the other end of the demon's chain and tugged along with him, and our pace doubled. We headed toward Zephyr's tent and the massive stone wall.

"I'm going to open the door. It goes without saying that you can't tell anyone how I do it. Not that it matters. Only someone with royal blood can open it. You got him?"

I glared and tugged hard on the demon's chains, forcing it to trip over itself and slam head first into the cold stone, jarring it under my feet.. I felt badly because it was a person once, but I didn't feel *too* badly. I'd just found Oleria only to lose her again. This was a thing now. Not a person. Not a person ever again.

Zephyr used the timing of the demon's fall to quickly turn and press both of his palms against the wall. A deep rumbling filled the tunnels, and the door separated in the middle just enough to accommodate the width of a person.

A trim person.

I didn't think I was claustrophobic, but staring into that tiny opening stretching out into a vast darkness made my stomach churn with unease.

"Push him through first. Keep him moving with this until I close the wall."

Zephyr pushed a long dagger hilt first into my hands—a dagger long enough to be considered a short sword. I stared at the blade and turned it, the flash of steel catching the light of the torches on the wall.

Could I use this on another living being?

A snarl came from the chains as the creature lunged at me. Without thinking, I swiped the sword at it, and it whined piteously as I caught it on the shoulder. Zephyr pushed the demon hard into the tunnel and gestured for me to follow. So, the answer was yes. I could definitely use it.

I held the dagger out like a beacon and kept the demon moving forward. The ground lurched and groaned once more as Zephyr closed the wall, sealing us in complete darkness. I tried and failed to quell the sudden wave of panic that surged through my veins.

"It's all right; the tunnel only goes to one place. Here, I'll switch with you."

I happily handed the dagger back over as he took my place behind the demon. The walls felt like they were pushing inward, but it had to be a figment of my imagination. Stone walls couldn't move. Still, scared and unsure, I balled my fist in the back of Zephyr's tunic, unable to handle separating from him for a second. His presence grounded me and kept me calm enough to keep moving forward.

Not that I could go back since he had closed the door behind us.

We walked at a good pace for about ten minutes until the demon came to an abrupt halt. I only knew this because Zephyr stopped short, and I nearly ran into him. The creature whined and snarled at us.

"All right, it would actually really help me out if you could hold it at knifepoint while I took the chains off."

Reluctantly, I took the blade back blindly, tentatively touching the edges to orient myself to where the point was. Wouldn't it be a laugh if I accidentally stabbed Zephyr or myself in the darkness?

I shuffled forward nervously.

"Hold right there. Just be ready to swipe at it if you hear it lunge."

Right. If I heard it lunge. Zephyr brushed past me, the clanking of chains confirming he was at least doing something. Zephyr swore and I pushed the blade forward a bit, hitting something soft and yielding. Terrified I'd stabbed him I pulled back, but the demon shrieked.

"There! Step back!"

As I did, I felt Zephyr go forward, and he must have shoved the demon hard. Its screams fell and descended, ringing out for a long time until they faded and I could no longer hear them.

"Was that ... is there a ..."

"Massive pit we toss all the demons into once they change? Yeah. The opening is a few feet in front of you, so don't take any steps forward."

Oh. Ok. Sure. No problem.

"Where is your hand? Don't move it as I take the sword back."

Fat chance of me making any movement until Zephyr told me to. Carefully, he took back control of the dagger and lightly pushed me back.

"All right, it's safe. Just walk back with me."

I grabbed his shoulder and dug my fingers into his muscles. My thoughts whirled as we walked. "You ... you do that to every Noble you get down here?"

His shoulders tensed beneath my fingertips. "What else would you have me do? Usually we toss them in a few hours before the change is imminent. Sometimes we don't have the calculations quite correct."

Frantically my head shook back and forth, even though I knew he couldn't see it. "That's worse! That just means they're still people when you chuck them into the pit! That's awful!"

Zephyr stopped and this time I did run right into him, banging my nose hard into his shoulder blades. I felt him whip around and throw my hand away.

"What am I supposed to do, Mari? Tell me! What would you do in my place? If you have a better idea, I would do it in a heartbeat!"

My lips parted, but nothing came out. I didn't have any better ideas. I just knew that this one wasn't right. The desperation in his voice was genuine, and shame rose within me. Who was I to condemn him? He was doing the best he could.

"Zephyr. I'm sorry," I whispered into the darkness.

If the sounds of his exaggerated and heavy footsteps were anything to go by, he whipped back around and stormed off. At a loss, I followed behind meekly. The cave walls shifted, whining and groaning in protest as he opened the door. Wordlessly, I passed through his disarmed traps and the quiet, dark stone passages, keeping my eyes on the uneven stone under my boots.

I passed the sick Nobles and the other women and their children, going straight to my tent without another word. I brushed his shoulder harder than necessary. He grabbed me, holding me still.

"Mari, I am sorry about your friend."

My throat tightened. Damnit, I wouldn't cry.

"This is ... this is hard. Trust me. I understand."

I nodded tightly, breaking away from his grasp and ducking under my tent flap as though it were a physical shield from the world and me. Inside, I was numb.

The mud people still starved. An entire enclave of

escaped women and their children lived below the kingdom like rats. Nobles came here to be trapped in the darkness for the rest of their lives, and the queen was still a raging bitch.

At least some things were consistent.

I fell face first onto my cot, burying my head in the small pillow and curling up in my blanket. Zephyr's shadow lingered outside of the tent flap, and for once, I wasn't sure what I wanted.

Should he come in? Should he go away? He was the reason my friend died ... or was he? My thoughts were such a jumbled mess.

"Mari. Can I come in?"

At least he asked. Zariah would have just barged in.

I sat up on my cot as he peeked his head into my tent. I wiped my nose and sniffed hard, waving him inside.

In a few quick strides, he made it to my cot, and went down on one knee in front of me. His full lips turned down at the sight of tears on my face, one thumb grazing gently against my skin as he wiped them away.

"Hey. I get it. We both—"

I seized him in a hug, unable to sort the chaotic emotions swirling in my head and hurt. He did get it, didn't he? We'd both grown up unwanted and unloved. We were trash from the mud quarter that was expendable. The lights from the lanterns flickered once, the metal shapes groaning against their iron brackets as a stray breeze sliced in from somewhere. The lanterns swayed back and forth before settling again into stillness.

His arms slowly settled on the tops of my shoulders, his grip light and unsure. Oh fuck, now I'd gone and made him uncomfortable!

I pulled away, flushed red. "Sorry. I need to get a grip. Sorry."

He blinked at me, his face blank and completely unreadable. "Yes. Well. I just wanted to offer my condolences, as mentioned, and ensure you were all right. Would you like something to eat? I have a bit of jerky here in my satchel."

I put a hand on his as he fumbled in the pouch at his side. "No thanks. Just ... just knowing you cared to check on me was really nice."

I smiled gently, and he met it with another oddly detached look that slowly curled into a small grin of his own.

"Good. I would like us to be friends. I feel like we could help each other out quite a bit," he said softly. Gods, it was strange to see Zion and Zariah staring back at me when it wasn't actually Zion or Zariah. He left me alone in my tent.

The weight of everything came crashing down on me at once. So many dead girls. So many dead Nobles. And why? For some curse no one knew the cause of?

Hot tears leaked down my cheeks, and for only the second time in my life, I didn't try to stop them. I wasn't in the mud quarter or at court any longer, so there was no one I needed to be strong for. In the privacy of this tent, no one would know if I broke down.

So I did.

I cried for Oleria, who'd found her own freedom even though it cost her so much, only to have it literally ripped away by a demon that Zephyr or Shava could have killed before they even changed. I cried for my mother, who was alone in the palace with only Ell to look after her. I cried for my friends and everyone in the mud quarter, all of us trapped by circumstance and forced to dance to the queen's song.

My head shot up. That was the end game, wasn't it? If I could take down the queen, I could return to the palace. We could figure out a better way to deal with the Noble curse, and Zariah and Zion wouldn't be forced to kill anymore.

All right. Tonight I would mope in my bed. I'd cry and mourn the loss of Oleria and the innocence of my friends, but only until morning.

Then I'd start planning a rebellion.

CHAPTER
FOUR

It was Shava's turn to pause outside of my tent the next morning, and after dressing, I opened the flap and held it for her.

My path forward was clear. Oleria was dead. I was determined to find Wisteria and ensure no one else died due to Shava or Zephyr's negligence, indifference, and stupidity. I hadn't really decided what letting a bunch of Nobles who would quickly become rapid demons hang out with young kids and scared women qualified as, so I labeled it as all of the above.

Hopefully, Shava would want to join me on my adventures, just like old times.

"Did you know her well? That ... girl." Shava began, sitting on the edge of the cot and looking around the tent as she spoke.

That girl?

"Oleria," I spat out, then softened. "I guess not. We were only in the castle for a week or two. All the girls bonded. Kind of."

Shava snorted, but I ignored the slight. Was she trying to find fault with everything I said and did? It was unlike her. I decided to try another tactic.

"Zephyr is incredible. He's done all of this," I said instead, gesturing around me vaguely. As predicted, her eyes lit up.

A smirk curled at the corner of my mouth. "I can see why you fancy him. He's much more charismatic than the princes. Probably due to his more humble background."

Not that it was Zion or Zariah's fault that they were part spoiled prince. It couldn't be helped.

A small grin cracked Shava's face. "Yeah. He's incredible. He knows what it's like to struggle, you know?" She sighed, leaning back onto her hands on my cot. "So few people understand."

That was something I could relate to.

"Look at us. We both found probably the only men who aren't crusty Nobles or degenerate mud boys." She giggled a bit at that, and for a brief flash of a moment, I was eight and she was twelve, confessing how she'd escaped an older man by punching him in the *you-know-where*.

Just as quickly, the memory dissipated. Those days seemed like a lifetime ago.

"Remember when you broke a boy's nose for that wheel of cheese? That was amazing," Shava said.

Oh, I remembered. "It was the first time I'd ever hit someone." A grin of satisfaction came to my face just remembering the shocked look on the boy's face.

I wasn't sure how long we stayed in my tent reminiscing, but eventually my rumbling stomach brought us out into the corridor. Shava waved goodbye, muttering about having to 'get ready.' I strapped my new fire materials to my waist and set out. A small tray with a slab of Zephyr's meat and a slightly rotted apple awaited me in front of my tent, and I swiped it thankfully, inhaling the whole thing in a minute. I set it just inside my tent flap, determined to give it back later. For now, I had work to do.

I stomped down the hall to where the twenty or so women and children lived, surprised to see Zephyr among them. He was playing ball with a small group of kids. They shrieked with delight as he made a dramatic movement to kick the ball, then purposefully flipped over on his back and fell to the ground. He grinned as the kids shrieked with laughter and all fell on top of him in a dog pile.

A corner of my mouth twisted up before I could help it. I couldn't imagine Zariah or Zion playing with children. Then again, Zephyr didn't have to worry about accidentally turning into a dragon and roasting everyone alive. Wait ... that meant the curse was centered around the queen specifically and not the royal family! Otherwise Zephyr would have been affected as the king's son. Right?

Another step closer to reaching the top of this mystery! Too bad the staircase of this curse seemed to have thousands of steps.

"Ah! Mari! Good. I'm glad you came."

Zephyr good-naturedly shook off the children as he approached me, seemingly without a care in the world. He acted as if the next corridor down there weren't a bunch of sick men and women who could turn into blood-thirsty savages and skin alive each kid here before we could blink. The anger inside me boiled. Just last night, my friend had died. She'd died because of his foolish hope that everyone could be saved somehow.

I crossed my arms over my chest and waited.

Seeing I was still just a tad irate, his grin dropped and he got to the point. "Shava and I will be out today. She'll be going outside the wall, so I'll return first. Are you able to keep watch over things? It is nice having someone else here so we don't always have to take turns with who goes out."

He flashed me a winning grin, but I wasn't susceptible to his charm. Not after last night. All the smiles in the world wouldn't wash away the sight of Oleria's mangled and torn body.

"Fine," I muttered, glancing at the ground.

Zephyr clapped his hands together. "Good, good. We will leave shortly. Thank you."

His gear was already strapped to his body, and Shava detached herself from another woman and gave her a hug goodbye before giving me a jaunty wave.

So my agreement had clearly been anticipated. That annoyed me. What was I supposed to do if someone else changed? We could all be slaughtered like livestock!

I had to do something. Drastic action must be taken. Sweat dripped down my back at the very thought.

I gave it a few minutes after they left before I cupped my hands around my mouth, wanting to ensure Zephyr and Shava were gone and wouldn't return to interrupt my plans. Zephyr and I working together could be great, but he definitely needed someone to challenge his ideas, and Shava wasn't about to do it. So it was up to me.

"Everybody out here! Announcement!"

Most people were already outside their tents, working on menial chores or tending children, but I waited a minute until they all moved closer and a few yawning mothers joined us from their tents.

"Listen up. After yesterday's little accident, we're changing things. All of you need to pack your shit and move. We're switching quarters with the Nobles. Let's go."

A hand landed on my back and I whirled around, only for Wisteria's wide eyes to meet mine. Her hair was still dirty blonde with copper highlights, though a bit oily and unkempt in a rough braid. Otherwise she looked good, and unharmed.

"Mari! I must have been sleeping when you arrived!"

Part of me wanted to pick her up and squeeze her tight, never letting go. The other part of me was afraid to get too close: she'd just end up dying like the others. I shook my head. "I'm changing a few things. Piss poor management got Oleria killed. As long as I'm down here, that shit won't happen again."

Wisteria gawked at me, but I moved on down to the Nobles' quarters. Her footsteps pounded behind me.

"Everyone who's able, up and at 'em! We're moving!" Heads poked out at me, but about a dozen people didn't move at all. A handful of five or so Nobles gathered their things, the look of misery in their eyes so raw it made me pause.

"I'll help," Wisteria declared, carefully ripping

down a few tents and folding the canvases. "Let's get the tents folded up first. If you have any personal belongings, take them. We can work on moving the sick ones last."

I nodded, inwardly pleased to have some support. I gestured over my shoulder for the sick Nobles to follow me. Those that could, anyway.

We walked the short path back to where the women and children were. They either didn't take me seriously or thought they'd had more time because no one had moved. Their terrified faces at seeing the sick Nobles behind me had them scurrying, though.

"What, do you think this is a game? Grab your shit and go, or I'm giving you to a Noble." I jerked my thumb over my shoulder for emphasis. A few of the children cried at seeing the gray, ashen skin of the Nobles, but I grit my teeth and ushered them forward.

The women rushed to tear down their own tents and gather supplies, making huge piles in the middle of the corridor.

"Thanks," I said to no one in particular, though varying looks of anger were directed my way. Time to nip that in the bud.

"This whole arrangement is backward. The Nobles need to be closer to the door so they can be more safely contained and don't have to pass through your camp once they change," I patiently explained. The huffy looks lessened a bit after that.

It took an hour or so, but soon everyone had moved. The sick Nobles who were able helped Wisteria and me drag the unconscious to their new tents, and soon each Noble was situated next door to Zephyr,

Shava, and me, with the women and children on the outside edges.

Now came the hard part, but the necessary part.

As soon as the last woman scampered away, I searched Zephyr's tent and found the ridiculously long knife from last night. I would go tent to tent, finding any sick Noble who was conscious and sane. It wouldn't be easy, but it needed to be done.

I steeled my nerves, and threw back the canvas flap of the first tent in the row. Inside was a young Noble. Too young. He was sitting up in his cot, staring out at nothing. His blonde hair was turning as gray as his skin, his face haunted and full of pain.

"I begged the bastard prince to do it," he began, smiling when he saw the knife at my side. "He refused. I tried to attack his girlfriend, to goad them into thinking I was changing. It didn't work. It just earned me a back so bloody I can't even sleep now," he complained bitterly, his blue eyes glowing against his ashen complexion. Scabs and scales started at his neck and covered him from wrists to ankles.

"I heard the girl screaming last night. I don't want to do that to anybody," he continued softly. "Will you do it?"

I glanced at the knife in my hands. "I want to grant your wish, but I've never done it before."

He chuckled. "I don't want it to be an agonizing mess either. Got any wine? I could get pissed off my ass. Shouldn't hurt as much."

The man tried to put on a brave face, but the fear was palpable in the way his hands shook around his ratty blanket.

"No wine. Sorry," I muttered. What was I thinking? How could I do what needed to be done?

"Well ... maybe just stab me in the heart, hard and fast. No regrets." He threw his blanket off of him and rolled onto the dirty floor, so he wouldn't bleed all over the blanket and ruin it.

The thoughtfulness he had about his own death left me paralyzed. This couldn't be the right way. But what else could I do?

"All right. I'm sorry."

He gave me a wistful smile. "Me too."

I kneeled over him and raised the knife.

Only to have the air knocked out of me as I was bodily thrown away. The knife skittered across the stone floor noisily.

"What the actual *fuck*?" Zephyr roared at me, standing over me as pissed and angry as I'd ever seen his half-brothers. "I realized I forgot my knife, and I came back to chaos! You've upset everyone! The women are crying, the children are terrified, and there are Nobles crawling all around my tent!"

I shot to my feet, indignant. I understood his anger; he was just trying to protect his people. But he was blind to the damage it was doing to the others, who were *also* his responsibility. You couldn't be blind to the torment of some and not others. This was how I'd prove my worth; this is how I'd be useful to the cause.

"Oleria died because you're too much of a coward to do what needs to be done." I gestured wildly at the man on the floor. "He begs for death. He wants it! Why won't you give it to him? Why do you refuse death with dignity, and instead pass a sentence of long, painful suffering in the pit?"

The man gasped behind me, and I whirled around. "Oh? The bastard prince didn't tell you? When you finally change, he'll wrap you in chains and drag you into a dark pit with a hundred other savage demons down there. Didn't he tell any of you that?"

Perhaps I was being a tad cruel, but the sick Nobles deserved a choice in their fates, and they deserved to have their choices honored. They should at least be able to choose if they wanted a quick death, or a slow, agonizing one in the darkness.

Zephyr ignored the speechless Noble as he grabbed me, dragging me out of the tent and slamming me up against the stone wall. His sudden anger and strength took me by surprise. Where was the gentle leader who had just played with children?

"You had no right to come here and disrupt everything. Get out!"

"You have no right to play god down here, like a prince of rats!" I spat back in his face, my knee going directly into his groin. He dropped me like a bad habit, and I jumped out of his reach. He stayed on the ground for a moment before collecting himself, pity and sadness in his eyes.

I didn't like that. I wanted anger. I wanted violence. I wanted him to fight me, and make his argument. Instead, he picked up the dagger, and advanced toward me.

"Where's Shava?" I asked, nervousness creeping into my veins.

"Out," he grit. "She'll be sad to hear about you, but she's used to friends dying. Go back to your little castle and your dragons, and forget about us."

We stalked around each other in a circle like two

wary predators. How had it all gone south so badly? I didn't miss how we'd turned so that I was facing the tunnel leading back up the surface, and his back was to the massive wall that led to the demons. He was pushing me out. He didn't actually want to fight me. That gave me hope.

Which meant maybe I could beat him. But not yet. I had to at least try to get him to see reason, first.

"Zephyr, I'm trying to help. You said we could work together. This isn't working together."

His eyes narrowed. "Working together, yes. Trying to lead a revolt? I don't think so. My entire life people have tried to take what was mine. I won't let some stupid mud girl do it now!"

My jaw dropped at the insult. Perhaps he was more like his half-brothers than I'd thought.

A child cried somewhere not far from me, reminding me of my purpose. Zephyr's motivations were blurring.

"You don't want to help anyone other than yourself," I accused him, wondering how he'd react, and beginning to suspect something. Zephyr lived down here like a little king among the poor and sick, but did little to end anyone's actual suffering or break the curse.

What did Shava see in him?

Slowly I backed away, not entirely convinced he'd just let me go back up to the palace.

"The only reason I don't throw you into the demon pit is because Shava is fond of you, and it's tedious to deal with her tears." Zephyr gestured with his knife to the tunnel behind me. "You have sixty seconds to get out of my sight. I even left the door open for you. One. Two—"

Angry tears filled my eyes but it would be stupid to fight him in his domain. It would be stupid to upset the women and children. I'd learned long ago in the mud quarter there was no honor or pride when it came to winning a fight. Running away was usually the best choice. You wouldn't be able to run for food or water the next day if you got yourself beat up, after all.

I just wondered why Shava had forgotten the same lessons.

With Zephyr's taunts in my ear, I turned and ran, past the moans of the shifting Nobles, and headlong into the tunnel as the rush of water roared around me. I didn't know water could be so loud until Shava had first brought me here. That was likely the reason I didn't know the demon was behind me until it wrapped a hand around my ankle and brought me down.

"AH!"

I twisted around on my back and kicked blindly. The face of the Noble who'd begged me to kill him minutes ago moved toward me in a jerky panic, his blonde hair the last remnants of his human self that hung on. His eyes were hungry and glazed, and it was clear he didn't have control over himself.

A sob left my throat as I landed a kick directly into that confused, ravaged face, and he fell to the side toward the dark river. The demon roared in anger and panic as his fingers desperately dug for purchase in the stones, fingernails cracking and bleeding as the river worked to sweep the lower half of his body away in the current.

Zephyr stalked toward us and paused as he glared at the demon hanging on, judgment in his eyes. That pissed me off the most.

"Fucking end it then!" I screamed at him, flat on my back and bleeding from my ankle where the demon had scratched at me.

Zephyr ignored me and continued to watch the demon struggle to fight against the raging current. An odd, fascinated gleam shone from his eyes as he stood inches away but did nothing, the demon scrabbling and biting to survive, but quickly losing his grip.

With one last shriek, the water took him, and he disappeared under the white rapids without a sound.

Something was wrong with the way Zephyr had watched him die—in a calculated, clinical way. I scrambled to my feet as he snapped his head around to me next, and at that moment, I had no idea if he'd still let me go or throw me into the water, too.

Zephyr wasn't who I thought he was. It had been a lie. Whether or not it was projected by him, or made up by my own desperate mind, it wasn't true. It hurt to realize I was wrong yet again. Would I always misjudge so badly?

Who was he?

I wasn't going to stick around to find out.

Blindly, I ran down the tunnel, trying to stay as close to the middle as I could in the darkness. When the sound of rushing water finally faded and the incline went up, up, up, I still didn't relax.

I did not relax even when I burst out of the entrance and saw glimmering stars in the sky, and not when the same rope I'd used to escape my room still hung from the rock, dangling in front of me like a cruel joke.

I wrapped the fabric around my wrist.

"Hey! You!"

A Fireguard rounded the corner and saw me, and as if things couldn't get any worse, another one was only steps behind him. And a third. And a fourth.

"Is that the dragon girl?"

"Fuck, fuck, fuck." I spat.

I had no choice but to drop the rope and flee back into the tunnel, their surprise at seeing me the only reason I was able to dart behind the rocks and into the darkness of the secret path.

"Where'd she go?"

The Fireguards blindly lunged toward the large rocks, and I knew it was only a matter of time before they found the open crevice between the rocks, and came after me. Had the iron gate been shut behind me? I didn't want to lead them inside!

I patted myself down wildly, but I already knew I had no weapon. Zephyr's long knife had been knocked away. Reaching down to the ground, I determinedly wrapped my fingers around a large rock.

My lip quivered, but I didn't have a choice. If the Fireguards discovered this tunnel, then they'd discover the Nobles and the women and children. If these four didn't die, countless more would.

Probably for the best.

I lurked in the darkness behind a rock, trying to even my breaths and form a plan. I'd have to strike the first one hard enough to knock him unconscious and immediately hit the second. With two down, my chances were better, but still not great against trained guards.

My eyes closed and a breeze lifted the stray hairs around my head. I raised the rock over my head and waited. Footsteps drew closer and closer ... now!

A blade flashed and I stumbled backwards, taken off guard as Zephyr lunged from the shadows opposite of me, stabbing the first guard in the chest with his dagger. The man fell and he moved to the next, slitting his throat, then spinning under the large sword of the third man. As he came up, he sliced into the Fireguard's private parts, and I gasped at the savagery. The last man dropped his sword in fear, the clang as the blade hit the rock ringing loudly in my ears.

He turned and ran.

Zephyr laughed and gave chase, leaving me alone with the three dying Fireguards. Adrenaline flooded my body and I shook. I'd seen death before, but not this close, and not this savage.

In no time at all, the bastard prince returned.

"Move."

Zephyr gave me no warning as he pushed the last Fireguard back into the tunnel. The man tripped and fell over his fellow guards, blood pouring from his chest.

"What are you doing?" I demanded, not recognizing the high pitch of my voice. "Just end it already!"

Zariah laughed. "I've some experiments to try. I like experiments. I didn't tell you that. Didn't want to offend your sensibilities or lose your trust. Not that I need it. Run along now. I won't even be mad at you. Shava should return soon." Without sparing a glance at me, he took the long knife and plunged it straight into the last man's chest, dragging it across him like he was cutting him open alive. The man's screams echoed horrifically, and the other dying Fireguards moaned.

Cold terror leached into my veins.

"Zephyr! Stop—"

That odd, crawling sensation spread across my skin, just like the one from the old mine. White light flickered around Zephyr's skin, his eyes glowing in the darkness. Or was I simply imagining it?

He cut another line in the man's chest, uncaring of the torment he was causing. What the fuck was he doing?

"ZEPHYR!" I took a step toward him to stop this insane torture.

A dragon roared overhead, close enough to see the glow from its flames. Zephyr scowled, the odd light around him snuffed out like a candle. He growled in frustration and sliced the man's throat, grabbing him under his armpits and dragging him into the tunnel.

"Are you going to help? Or am I cleaning up your mess alone?"

Indignation welled in my veins. "*Your* mess," I muttered to myself, still in shock. Automatically, I moved to grab the next dead Fireguard, following Zephyr back to the tunnel with the water and watching as he callously kicked the bodies into the raging river with his boot.

Zephyr hesitated over the other two bodies, a manic glint in his eyes. One of the dragons (it was impossible to tell if it was Zariah or Zion) screeched again, even closer than before. Zephyr growled, but picked up the second dead guard from under the man's armpits and gestured with his head that I should take the feet.

Relief shot through my body. Zephyr was too nervous about the dragons to ... do whatever it was he had wanted to do and whatever he wanted to do certainly didn't feel good. We carried the second man over to the rushing rapids, and with a manic grin, Zephyr swung the body into the water.

Before I could blink, the last body was disappearing into the wet, black abyss, and I was covered in blood and shaking.

"What ... what do you mean by experiments? What were you going to do?" I asked. I was afraid of knowing, and yet ... I had to know.

Zephyr sighed, wiping his hands together as though we'd just completed a hard day's work together and not covered up brutal murders of good men who'd just been doing their jobs. He put a hand gently on my shoulder, looking so unlike the deranged killer from ten minutes ago that I wondered if I had imagined it.

"I grew up in the Seat, studying at the sides of great thinkers. There were historians who studied the past and healers who were looking toward the future. Do you know where the future of humanity resides?"

I shook my head dumbly, tense as his fingers dug into the muscles of my shoulder.

"*Magick*, dear. Your dragon princes and the queen rule not because they are the most wise or deserving, but because they have magick. Magick grants power. Power grants ... *everything*."

His voice was soothing and dark, and it was as if his words were a black lullaby trying to lull me to sleep or complacency. I hardened my heart and shook off his hand.

"You can't torture and kill people. Any magick that comes from that is evil, and you'll be cursed."

Zephyr laughed at me.

"Cursed? You mean how your little princes are cursed? Yes, it must be so terrible to have the ability to turn into a giant beast and destroy all your enemies in one fell swoop." He beat his fist into the palm of his hand for emphasis, his teeth grit together. His neck swiveled toward me, eyes glittering.

"How do you think medicines and treatments are developed, Mari? By simply theorizing? Or by human experimentation?"

My mouth went dry, and I had to lick my lips to get anything out. "I ... I wouldn't know. Mud girls don't get medical treatment."

A twisted grin curled at the corners of his mouth. "Touché. However, you're not stupid despite our shared background. You know I'm right. All knowledge and advancement comes at a cost. Would you really save one soldier if it meant one hundred others wouldn't die? Children, even?"

He gestured dramatically toward the rushing rapids. I couldn't help but wonder where all the bodies ended up. Did they eventually wash away to another kingdom, with the people who found them horrified and shocked? Were they given proper burials then or left to rot in the shallows? My stomach twisted. I didn't want to acknowledge what he implied, but in my heart it made sense.

Zephyr scoffed. "Next time, don't interfere. Maybe

you'll learn something." He turned and walked back into the darkness of the tunnels.

I found myself with no choice but to follow him.

We did the same to the other two men. When it was done, I was covered in blood and shaking. I was an accomplice trapped underground with a madman, and I only had a few more answers than when I'd left the castle balcony. One place had a queen determined to see me put under the ground, and yet under the ground, my soul lay cracked and bleeding. Which despot was worse?

Horrified, I realized I wasn't sure.

CHAPTER FIVE

"Hurry up, Mari. Wouldn't want to linger."
Zephyr's voice carried in the darkness ahead of me. Even though a sense of unease still tingled at the back of my neck, I rolled my eyes. He was the most dangerous thing in these tunnels, as far as I was concerned.

A sudden thought flipped my stomach. Did Shava know what he got up to? Maybe she could talk some sense into him! I had to put distance between us. I had to tell Shava.

Pushing my way past his shoulder, I led. He waited a few moments before stalking behind me. Neither of us said a word as we passed the new camp mothers and children . . . and the Nobles. I walked until I met the great stone wall with its tunnel to the dark nowhere: the dark pit where he sacrificed countless others.

"Nowhere to go, flower. You can't run from this."

I turned and Zephyr was only a few steps away,

blood crusting over his blade as he wiped it on his pants.

"It's unnecessary. It's cruel," I pleaded desperately, my hands fluttering uselessly like two dying birds. Like the last two dead guards we'd plunged into the abyss.

He rolled his eyes. "Death is all around us. Don't get squeamish now. My work will help humanity as a whole."

"Does Shava know?" I demanded. I still doubted she'd be with him if she knew the depths of his savagery.

He fucking laughed at me, like I was a child who didn't understand.

"Mari, don't you see that if I'm able to study magick and understand it, then we could use it to find a cure and end all of this. That's what you want, right?"

That didn't make any sense at all, and I felt trapped. "Any kind of magick that involves ... whatever you were doing . . . can't be good."

Zephyr sighed. "Ah, I believe you said 'evil,' didn't you?" He trapped me up against the stone wall, shoving his knife to the left of my head and into a crack in the stone. I squirmed, wondering how the mechanism worked to open it. I didn't care that it led nowhere; I just wanted to be alone, and away from him. The darkness would be a welcome break from his madness.

"What if the demons get out before you can stop them? Everyone in the kingdom is at risk! We should just—"

"Put them down like the animals they are?" Zephyr interrupted, an odd gleam in his eyes.

I blinked, wondering if he was finally starting to

understand. "I—I don't know! They're rabid! You saw that demon last night! You couldn't reason with it! If you let it, it would have torn through this entire camp unless someone killed it first! How can you risk the lives of children over those ... things? How could you kill those Fireguards like that? That wasn't fighting. It was torture!"

There was nowhere to go. My back was already up against the wall.

"So the children and the women's lives are more important than the Nobles' lives?" he asked, his face twisting with emotion.

"Well, I don't know, but it's what's best for everyone!" I argued back, not understanding why he couldn't see it. Was he trying to say the demons deserved just as much protection as the children? That didn't make any sense! He was the one who was trying to argue that sick experiments were necessary for the good of the whole! So why didn't he see it here?

"I don't understand," I mumbled again, mostly to myself. He must have taken it as a challenge, though, because he stepped right up to me and got in my face, the blade of his knife at my throat.

I closed my eyes and waited for the sharp feel of steel slicing through my flesh.

"You want to know why they deserve a chance? Why I *truly* want to study magick?"

I heard the rustling of fabric, and the strike never came. My eyes cracked open to see the arm that held the knife against my throat, the sleeves of his long tunic pushed up to his elbow.

Ashy, gray scales covered his wrists and upper arm. Faint and barely detectable, but they were there.

"You're—"

"A failed experiment," he growled at me, shoving me hard against the door again. My head smacked against the stone and I saw stars.

Stay awake. Fight.

"My diluted mud blood staved off the effects longer than any other Noble I've seen," he continued, anger and defiance in his eyes. "But it obviously wasn't enough. A Noble is a Noble. They're all cursed. Do we all deserve to die for something we don't understand? For something we have no part of? For something that happened two hundred years ago?"

A small gasp left my mouth. "You know what happened."

His curly black hair fell forward into his eyes, just like Zariah and Zion's. "Of course I know what happened. It's mud history—my history. Your history!"

It seemed stupid suddenly that we were fighting. With our dark hair and eyes, we could have been brother and sister. We should be working together and sharing information, not fighting and holding blades up to each other's throats.

"Zephyr, I'm sorry. Let's start over. I need to know about the curse. I know it has something to do with our people and how we were slaves."

He snorted. "You are a bed warmer for the prince. Possibly both, if what I hear is accurate. You can't be trusted. You'll return to the castle and rat us out."

My jaw dropped. "No more than Zariah or Zion would!"

He laughed. "Neither of them know exactly where we are. How could they when the queen could simply order them to tell her what they know? They know where the tunnel begins, but we have it laced with so many booby traps we'd hear the Fireguards screaming long before they reached us. How do you think you got here so quickly, and were able to race out without becoming a bloody smear on the wall? I disabled everything for you! Every time you travel with me or Shava, your path is clear. Try it now and see how far you get, you little weed."

I glanced down at his ashen wrist. "Zephyr, please. Tell me what you know before it's too late. Share your knowledge before it becomes lost. We don't have magick! We—"

"I WON'T CHANGE!" he screamed in my face, bits of spit flying from my nose and hitting my cheeks with how close he was. "THEY CAN BE SAVED, we just haven't figured out what to do yet! My cursed blood gives me magick, and I'll butcher a hundred Fireguards if that's what it takes to learn how to use it!"

It all came crashing together at once for me, and in the blink of an eye, I understood. Zephyr wouldn't kill the demons no matter how dangerous they were, because killing them meant giving up. If a demon died, in his mind, it meant he would die as well. Yet he was fine torturing others to suit his own needs and thirst for knowledge.

"Zephyr, I'm going to figure out how to break the curse. But you can't have these people living down here with the Nobles. If you won't kill them, then the people have to go."

His dark eyes met mine, flaring with anger. "You don't tell me what to do. No one tells me what to do. My entire life, everyone else has told me what to do.

My brothers have everything. I wonder if their dragons will feel it when you die?"

I whirled around and pressed my palms to the hard stone, looking for a lever or something that would indicate how it opened.

Zephyr snorted. "I told you, I'm the only one who can open it. Only royals can—"

His guffaws died in his throat as the wall slid open in the middle the moment my palms touched it. I darted inside as fast as I could, hearing his footsteps racing after me. Royals my ass. Perhaps it only opened for *our* people. Mud people.

"Close! CLOSE!" I screamed at the wall, slapping my hands up against it again. The underground groaned and shuddered, but began to close. Slowly. Too slowly.

I winced as Zephyr shoved his body toward me and only managed to get stuck. Horror bloomed in his eyes as the wall kept closing in, with him trapped in between.

"NO! OPEN BACK UP!" I screamed to no one, my palms scraping so hard against the stone that it left bloody trails in its wake. Something loud cracked in Zephyr's chest, but then mercifully, the walls went out again. Zephyr collapsed.

Sobbing, I pushed his body back out into the corridor until he was clear of the tunnel. He was unconscious, but still breathing. "SOMEONE HELP!" I screamed, then ducked back into the tunnel. On second thought, I darted back out and grabbed the long knife from his hands.

"Close," I breathed into the stone, ignoring the

sting in my hands. Darkness fell all around me, and the last thing I saw through the narrowing crack was Zephyr's eyes shooting open with a vicious and determined gleam.

CHAPTER SIX

Well, that hadn't been my plan at all. I'd wanted to secure the Nobles closer to the door and away from the healthy ones, and offer a way out for those who'd wanted it. Zephyr returning early put an end to that. And it'd spiraled out of control from there.

I sat down in the darkness of the tunnel, weighing my options. If I was going to escape, I might as well open the wall again and do it while Zephyr was hurt and not a threat to me. Then again, curiosity about the pit burned in me. Were the demons down there alive?

I suspected they were, and that there were other tunnels that connected to the old mines that they could use to travel in. How else would Zariah and I have uncovered nearly a hundred chittering demons that day?

I scooted forward slowly on my hands and knees, not wanting to risk falling down into the pit. My muscles burned and cramped from the uncomfortable position, but I wasn't taking any chances as my hand slid across the rough stone. I heard the demons before my hand reached out. I touched only empty air.

As I dragged my body closer, the sound of chittering and growls grew. I don't know what made me do it, but I gripped the edges of the hole with one hand and yelled down into the pit.

"Hello?"

The same pressure and feeling of unease I'd encountered in the cave with Zariah washed over me—a prickling sensation. It was as if my body were being covered in tiny insects. I tried to ignore it and push on.

"Anyone down there?"

A chorus of shrieks and screams met me, so loud and close that I pushed myself back away from the hole. I knew it was deep and they couldn't escape—otherwise Zephyr wouldn't have thrown them in there. But it was still terrifying.

"All right. So there's a lot of you down there."

I wondered just how many. And for how long? Did they eventually die? Find their way to the larger cavern?

"Mari? MARI! I know you're in there! GET OUT HERE NOW!"

Shava's muffled voice came from the other side of the stone, enraged. The pain in my chest had nothing to do with panic or anxiety. It was clear by the tone of her voice that I wouldn't be given a chance to explain myself or argue; she'd already chosen her side. Even if I did, why would she choose me over her lover boy? And to be honest, it looked bad, really bad. No doubt

Zephyr would fill Shava's head with stories about how I tried to murder everyone, including him.

And it was insane, wasn't it? How could I defend killing others even if it was for mercy and everyone's safety? Clearly they didn't understand it, or they would have done it already. Zephyr hadn't seen the desperation in the Noble's eyes. Shava hadn't seen the relief in the eyes of the women and children as I moved them further away from the Nobles who were turning.

Or perhaps they did see it and chose to ignore it.

I couldn't ignore it. I wouldn't ignore it.

Which left one option.

The walls and floor beneath me groaned with effort as the door slowly creaked open, Zephyr was conscious enough to open it for Shava. I let out an inappropriate giggle. If mud blood opened it, then so could Shava. Funny how Zephyr never mentioned that to her, eh?

"I can't believe you'd do this! I thought you were my friend!" Shava's voice grew louder, though still subdued by a dozen feet of rock, but becoming clearer as the pathway opened. Her whip cracked against the stone, further emphasizing the rift in our friendship.

I thought you were my friend, my mind whispered, but there was nothing for it. Before I lost my nerve I plunged forward.

I jumped into the pit.

Hands reached for me as I fell twenty feet, my fall broken by a multitude of writhing bodies. The moment their clammy skin came in contact with mine, they went feral, biting and scratching and trampling each other in their fervor to get to me. The thick crowd worked to my advantage—they attacked each other while I crawled underneath them, dragging myself into a dark corner and hoping I could act quickly enough to avoid getting my bones chewed. I threw my two satchels to the ground and dug in furiously, searching for the flint, striker, and charcoal shavings.

Perhaps it was the adrenaline making me hit the objects together with more force than necessary, or just luck, but after two strikes the sparks caught on the charcoal. Fumbling with one hand, I grabbed the dried grass and wrapped it lovingly around the tiny ember as my hands shook, breathing softly into it as Shava had done. The grass had barely burst into flame before I yanked the torch out and ripped the cloth cover off, stuffing it back into my satchel in case I needed something else to burn later.

I lifted the small flames to the torch, squinting as the torch burst into bright light. The squeals and screams of the demons became more frantic, the sound of claws scurrying away ringing all around me as they fled from the fire.

Good.

Now how long would it last?

Resolving to think about that another time, I took a moment to breathe and study my surroundings. This pit was large, but nothing like the cavern Zariah and I had explored. Tunnels led off in several directions, so at least the demons weren't trapped down here in a pit. It made me feel a bit better. The bones that crunched underneath my feet, however? They definitely didn't.

Would Shava realize she could open the doors and come charging after me?

No, I realized quickly. Zephyr had told her she couldn't, so I doubted she'd try. *She was probably too busy fussing over his broken nails and mussed hair,* I thought wryly.

Speaking of the demons, a few hadn't fled with the rest but simply stayed out of reach and gave me a healthy berth as they watched me with black, beady eyes. Since they weren't about to immediately chew me down to my bones, I took a moment to have a proper look.

Their skin was nothing but ash and charred, black crisps. Their eyes were just as black, their shining reflections in my torch the only reason I could see them at all. They wore decomposing scraps of whatever Noble clothing they'd had on when they'd turned. Gold threads hung frayed from old tunics, and precious gems hung haphazardly from their once rich dresses and adornments.

There was likely a fortune large enough to feed the entire mud district down here in the darkness. A few weeks ago, it would have made me angry; now it simply made me sad.

The demons ranged from emaciated to freshly turned. Two were gaunt with hollow cheeks and sharp bones poking out, while three others still had the plumpness of their old bodies, indicating they'd been thrown down here recently. Despite their lack of aggression, there didn't seem to be anything lurking behind their eyes. They all reminded me of mindless animals, shrinking in fear as I thrust my torch out at them for a closer look.

Except for one.

The gold necklace around its charred chest shone

and mocked me from the darkness. It was the demon. The one who'd killed my friend. Its frame didn't have the same, dirty look as the others, indicating it was fresh. The demon in question didn't shy away from my fire or act skittish. Rather, there was a keen, unnerving intelligence in its eyes as it looked at me.

"You killed Oleria," I accused, wanting desperately to be angry at the demon, but the rage wouldn't come. Deep down, I knew it wasn't this Noble's fault. I knew it had no choice, yet it'd been Oleria's choice to stay in this madhouse knowing the risks.

The demon shuffled forward, crouched awkwardly with its head bowed. I stood my ground, holding my breath. It whined, a grating, harsh sound that carried the sorrow of the kingdom in its tone. Something soft met my hand, the one not holding my torch. I glanced down as the demon shoved a small scrap of cloth between my fingers. Holding it up to my face, my throat tightened.

It was a length of gauze; the same gauze that had been wrapped around Oleria's burned hand.

An angry retort bubbled in my chest and my fist raised on its own volition to strike out. The demon made another pitiful noise and bowed its head, baring its neck to me, as if accepting whatever blow I would deal out.

Almost as if ... it was *sorry*.

My next breath was stolen from my lungs as the implications hit me. These weren't mindless beasts or dark creatures who needed to be put down like rabid dogs.

Not yet.

I eyed them all again. The emaciated, hungry ones

were the ones acting like feral creatures, fleeing in fear at my fire and yet unable to completely run away, driven by their hunger to stay near me in case I dropped dead. The ones gathered closer to me with unnerving sentience were full-bodied and fleshed out; fresh. Was it because they had been newly turned or because they were newly *fed*?

"Can you understand me?" I asked it softly, holding the bloodstained scrap of fabric close to my chest. The demon lifted its head cautiously, then gave a quick nod and shuffled forward, leaning its big, ashy head into my side and nuzzling it like a chastened dog.

This was weird, disturbing, and it changed everything.

What if they only were rabid at first as they changed? Or crazed only because they were down here slowly starving?

The thought made me ill ... poor Oleria! But there was nothing I could do to help her now.

I might be able to help everyone else, though. Including the demons.

My body itched and vibrated, no doubt due to the close proximity of some magick, just like it had when Zariah and I had visited the caves.

Urgh, Zariah and Zion. I didn't want to think about them now. There was too much between us, unspoken and spoken.

"Have you explored these tunnels at all? Do they lead somewhere?" I asked.

The demon gently grasped my index finger in its rough, ashy hand, and tugged me forward. The other demons followed like mindless hounds pulled along by their master.

Together we went down the tunnel on the left, the air cooler the further we went. It was odd; I was much less at fear down here with demons all around me than I had been upstairs with Zephyr, surrounded by the sick Nobles. There was a quiet restlessness down here and a steady feeling of purpose. Up there, there'd been nothing but despair and resignation.

The tunnel widened dramatically, and my strange honor guard of demons used the extra space to push around me, chittering excitedly like a bunch of children eager to show their mother a small treasure they found.

And small treasures they had in spades.

One demon pulled on my arm and pushed a small clay dragon into my hand, its fangs and gaping mouth stretched into a macabre grin. I gave him (because they were all 'hims' and not 'its') a shaky grin of thanks in return, and he bounded away only for another one to take his place.

Another demon tugged on the bottom of my tunic and pointed to the cave wall where there were long claw marks gouged into the wall, along with a few other items of note.

Artwork. Pictures.

I stopped and gawked, my demon guide slowing next to me as we all looked together. I squinted at it, then relaxed my eyes, trying to take in the crude markings as a whole rather than individually. That's when it started to make sense.

The markings were old and etched deeply into the wall. The dragon was easy to spot by its giant oblong body and the two wings. Lines spewed from its mouth, indicating fire. Stick figures cowered and ran beneath it, turning into a giant pile of squiggles and scribbles.

Ash.

"What is it you want me to see?" I asked quietly.

The demons around me were silent and staring. It was as if they knew that whatever was etched here was important, even if they weren't sure what it was. My demon guide tugged on my hand and pointed to the far left, and I raised my torch. The light illuminated another set of drawings; ones which seemed to precede this one. I ran my fingers over the etchings, swallowing heavily.

A crude figure of a woman was on the far left, standing over a cluster of figures working. The woman had an angry look on her face. The second drawing showed her with her arms outstretched, more lines and shapes flowing from her fingers toward a group of stick figures with flowing robes and hair. One of them wore a crown. The next picture had the same figures bent over and contorted, crying out. The figure with the crown twisted with them. The last picture showed the people turning into monsters, and the figure with the crown into a dragon. The final picture was the one I'd already seen, with the dragon flaming and destroying everything in its path.

I remembered the 'fantastical stories' Zephyr had mentioned before I'd run, the pieces flying together in my mind. I said it out loud more for my benefit than the demons, but it felt nice to have an audience that wasn't sneering at me or trying to lord their knowledge and skills over my head.

"There was a witch," I began slowly. The demons went still, like children gathered around me to hear a campfire story. "She saw the slaves working in the mines, and cast a spell that turned the Nobles into demons, and the princes into a dragon."

I stared at the second picture. It made sense when I said it out loud, but it didn't feel right. I was missing something.

"The dragon came to the mines and ... and killed all the slaves there. That's what shut down the mines." My voice broke a little, and I scarcely dared to believe it. Zariah had sworn he hadn't done it. Had he lied, or had it been Zion who'd gone on a massive killing spree? Both of them agreed Zion had the least control over his dragon between the two of them, but I just couldn't imagine one of my boys killing in cold blood like that, even if it was ordered by the queen. It didn't fit!

And the timeline ... these carvings were old. So old.

"Thanks for showing me," I told the demons. "Is there anything else?"

They shuffled around me as if in a hive mind mentality, herding me gently down the tunnel until we emerged into the same large cavern Zariah and I had explored.

The old mines.

More demons erupted from crevices and pits as we entered, emerging like ants. There were hundreds ... no, thousands! They shrieked and moaned and cried out like they had before, but it didn't fill me with fear like it did last time. Now I understood. They were hungry. They were confused. They were hurting.

Together, they rushed me to sniff and poke at me, and again I was reminded of large, dirty dogs. No, I had to stop thinking like that. These were people, just changed. It was demeaning and awful to think of them like dogs, like how the queen thought of my people.

A short demon frowned at me and grabbed my hand, tugging me toward one of the many tunnels. Only about a dozen demons came with us, the rest falling back and staying in the large cavern.

We walked for what felt like ages, until the air grew hot and stifling, and the stone floor under my feet inclined sharply and gave way to dirt. Great large boulders met us at what appeared to be a dead end.

"What—" I began, cut off when the small demon bounced forward, slipping easily between a gap in the middle of the rocks that wasn't obvious when you looked at it. I squeezed between it and the demon, who refused to take another step further. I stumbled into a familiar opening, daylight hitting me in the face as I emerged from the darkness.

I recognized this. I used to hide here as a child. We were in the mud quarter, in one of the many old mine entrances that everyone had thought blocked.

The demon behind me whined, taking care to stay out of the sun. My eyes weren't ready for the brightness either after such an extended time underground. I backed up into the tunnel again just to take it all in.

"I don't understand," I began. "What keeps you from leaving these tunnels? Even if you don't attack, you could still escape. What keeps you here?"

"Something has to be keeping you here," I insisted. "What is it?"

"Something? More like someone."

There was a shuffling sound from behind me and the demon fled, abandoning me as his shrieks and squeals disappeared into the darkness, fleeing from the new arriver as fast as he could.

I whipped around to find the queen standing at the entrance, dressed in fighting leathers and smiling like I was a fat, juicy hunk of meat that had just been handed to her on a warm plate.

"Hello, mud girl."

CHAPTER
SEVEN

Seeing the queen dressed in anything other than her immaculate robes was jarring in itself. To see her here in the mud quarter without any of her Fireguards? Mind-blowing. The glare like she'd prefer to have my insides on my outside was familiar and oddly comforting. At least some things never changed.

I still took a step back when she moved toward me, prepared to use my torch as a club if I had to.

Her tinkling laughter grated against my nerves. "Still as uncouth as ever. You mud people are all the same."

Rage coursed through my veins. "Apparently, you like it, seeing as you keep bedding us," I shot back.

Her eyes narrowed. "I see your time down here hasn't taught you any manners. Aren't you wondering what I'm doing out here, all alone and defenseless?"

Defenseless was a word I'd never use in regards to her. Yet, I kept my mouth shut.

"I wondered where you'd run off to, you know. Your little band of friends and family were distraught, so it was clear they didn't know. But my sons were oddly stoic through it all. Strange, considering how attached they were to you."

Despite the heat in the air, a chill went up my spine, and goosebumps burst across my skin.

"I figured they knew where you'd scampered off to, like the rat you are. And I was right." She stuck her nose triumphantly in the air, smoothing down her immaculate white braid with one hand. "And what a secret I stumbled across! Not only did I discover where you'd gone, but I exposed an entire network of traitors and spies, ferreting out these dangerous creatures underneath my kingdom instead of putting them down like the crazed monsters they are."

"They're not monsters," I spit out. "They're sane, still. They're just hungry. If—"

"That will be the last time my sons hide things from me," the queen interrupted darkly. She tutted, waving a finger at me.

"What did you do to Zariah and Zion?" I asked, hating the small tremor in my voice.

She laughed. "They can't disobey me, can they? Don't worry your muddy little head. No punishment I could give would be greater than the despair they already feel knowing they'd betrayed your location to me."

A deep ache flared in my chest, but I ignored it. I could be sad later. Right now, I had to stay alert. I had to survive—just like always.

"Well then? You finally going to kill me?" I put my hand under my chin in mock thought. "Oh, that's right. You never do your own dirty work." I looked around in exaggeration, my free arm up toward the sky. "Well? Where are the boys?"

The queen smiled, and my blood turned to ice. "Perhaps you're right," she purred at me, circling around and eyeing me up and down like a tasty snack. "It has been a while since I've had a chance to ... *stretch my wings.*"

My brain finally made the missing connection it had been missing this whole time, one I'd been utterly blind to, but it made so much damn sense now that I'd finally fucking thought of it. My mind shut off as my body took over, instincts rushing forward as I threw myself to the side, dropping my torch and rolling to dodge under the mass of silver scales that exploded in front of me.

The queen roared as she transformed, the ground shaking as dirt and debris fell from the tunnel. Should I run back into it for safety, or would the queen collapse it all and crush me? Indecision tore me in two.

I crawled forward out of the tunnel and gawked at the massive silver dragon in front me. She was a twin to Zariah and Zion, but all silver where they were gold. That included her eyes. Where the light hit her scales, shimmering patches of green and blue winked at me.

Of course she was a dragon. She was a crowned figure in the cave etching. She was the one originally cursed, not my boys! So why reveal herself now? Why—

I ducked and threw myself against the tunnel wall as her spiked tail swung at me haphazardly, but she wasn't aiming for me. In fact, she wasn't even looking at me. What was she doing?

Her massive body launched directly toward the mud quarter. Realization brought dawning horror as her intentions became clear. She wasn't going to kill me. She wasn't going to maim me. The queen was going to enact her revenge by doing something much, much worse.

"NO!" I screamed, darting out of the tunnel and running toward the rows of houses that made up the mud quarter. My home.

The dragon shrieked with what could have been laughter, and threw me back into the tunnel with one sweep of her giant tail. This time, I didn't dodge. I hit the stone wall hard and collapsed to the ground, too stunned to move. I wasn't bleeding, though, just felt like I'd been run over by the food cart. *Get up,* I screamed at my body. *GET UP!*

I staggered to my feet blinded with pain, but it was too late. Screams and cries for mercy met my ears as I stumbled out of the tunnel and laboriously climbed up to level ground. Heat and ash swirled around me and I sobbed, knowing it was already too late but hoping beyond hope the familiar outline of the mud quarter would greet my eyes when I finally made it over the lip.

Devastation met my gaze.

In a few seconds, the queen had razed the entirety of the mud quarter, reducing it to a hollowed out, charred pit. She couldn't burn the mud homes, but she could burn the people and everything inside of them. Bodies lay strewn everywhere, skin black and blistered from the heat and flames. Any scrap of cloth was on fire. Flames licked intensely at whatever it could, whether that be food, blankets, or skin. The dragon was nowhere to be seen.

That's why the queen had revealed herself—there would be few survivors to tell tales, and if anyone did, they wouldn't be believed. Who would believe filthy little mud rats, after all?

Cries and moans filled the air, a cacophony of pain and suffering so overwhelming I had to take a step back.

"That hurts much more, doesn't it?"

I jumped as the queen whispered in my ear, falling to one knee as the pain in my body doubled at the sudden, unexpected movement.

"This is what you deserve for coming into my home and trying to upset the balance. You can't win. You will never win. Mud rats always lose. And if I ever catch a whiff of you near my boys or my palace again, it'll be your mother, father, and brother next. Oh, how I'd love to slit his throat while he thrusts inside me. I will have more sons, and there won't be any mud girls left to spread their legs for them and poison their minds against me."

A crazed laugh broke from my lips. "You're aging! How much longer do you think you'll be able to have children?"

Perhaps it wasn't the smartest thing I could say, but I was past caring. The queen was obviously going to kill me. Might as well make it count.

Her pale skin flushed pink. "I should kill you, but if I did it now it would be over too quickly. I want you to suffer. I want my boys to watch you cry out in pain, and get on their knees to beg me to stop. And then I won't. I'll go slower, fingernail by fingernail, until you have no voice left to scream, and your eyes glaze over with insanity. Only then will I release you back to my boys, as a living husk and reminder of what happens when they think they can get around direct orders."

My jaw dropped. "Damn."

Her eyes narrowed. "As I said, I don't have the time now. I must be presentable for the ball tomorrow. If you are still here in the next coming days, I will hunt you. I will imprison you. And then the fun will truly begin."

She took a step forward, and I took a step back. It was crazy that Zephyr wasn't her true son; they were two fucked up, crazed peas in a pod.

"Goodbye, mud girl."

The queen walked away, leaving me with the ruins of all my hopes and dreams. The king had been right; I couldn't save them. I couldn't even save myself! All I'd done was bring on more pain and suffering. Why hadn't I listened to him? Why had I been so headstrong and stubborn? I'd thought I could do what the king himself had failed at.

Stupid little flower. All flowers die. You can't even eat them. Weak, useless little things.

I fell the rest of the way to the ground, barely able to catch myself with my arms.

Shock. You're in shock.

It was all over. The queen had won.

Crawl back into the tunnel. Lay down and die. Let the demons eat you. Let Zephyr and Shava find you. You don't deserve to live after what you've done.

A shrill scream sliced through the air, drawing my attention. Painstakingly, I lifted my head, watching as the little girl I'd seen on the day of my reaping run by me, screaming with her dress on fire.

I wasn't done. I might have made a mistake and under-

estimated the queen, but I could fix this. I could still help.

Adrenaline fueled my body and pushed aside the pain as I leaped up, chasing after her. I plowed into her and gathered her into my arms, both of us rolling on the ground and coming to a rough stop. The flames were gone, beat out by our antics. Both of us gasped for air, breathing hard.

"Are you all right?" I croaked. Smoke was everywhere. If the heat or fire didn't get everyone, the smoke just might.

"I want my momma!" the girl wailed, wrenching away from me and running off again. I didn't have the strength to chase after her, and the rush of adrenaline was gone, leaving me numb and exhausted.

It would be easy to just close my eyes and let the world take over. Whatever happened to me, happened. I was tired of trying. Tired of caring. Wouldn't it be nice to just sleep?

My eyes closed and I yawned even as the world went to hell around me. Vaguely, I registered the shrieks and cries of demons, and more blasts of heat. Was the queen destroying the demons now? That would be like her ...

I wanted to care. I wanted to help.

I'd helped too much already. My help caused this mess.

The pain in my side reached a crescendo. I hadn't heard anything crack when I hit the tunnel wall, but maybe I'd just missed it. It would be fair play if I suffered the same injury I'd accidentally given Zephyr.

At least I wasn't bleeding, right?

A large shadow descended down toward me and I passed out right as it reached me.

CHAPTER EIGHT

I opened my eyes.

Cloudless sky with no dome and no glittering stars greeted me, and it was quiet. Pain pulsed in waves through my side, but not as badly as before. I was half propped up on something warm, while something—or someone—else had their arms wrapped around me.

"Mari? Are you all right?"

I blearily tilted my head back, finding those silver eyes with a tinge of green. The queen's silver scales flashed in my mind and I recoiled, remembering everything that had happened. Shame raced through my body, warming my cheeks. I'd given up and done nothing to help as she'd destroyed my entire quarter. Hot tears gathered in the corner of my eyes.

"Hey, it's OK. Ssh."

The arms around me tightened.

"She can cry if she needs to. Gods above, I would if it were me," argued a second voice.

I turned into Zion's chest and squeezed him, letting the emotions overtake me as I sobbed into him.

"It's OK. Take your time. We're here."

I wanted to be mad at them. Or at least one of them. We'd argued the last time I'd seen Zariah. I knew logically it was unimportant now; that his actions had spoken far louder than his words that night in my rooms.

But they still hurt me, and he needed to know that.

"Zariah?" I asked, my voice raspy and dry.

He leaned closer into me, and I struck before he could react.

SMACK.

My hand collided hard with his cheek and he flinched back, shocked. Hot tears gathered in the corner of my eyes, all of the hurt and embarrassment rushing back as if he'd just said those awful words moments ago instead of a few days.

"You people always see the worst in everything. That's why you're slaves,"

Zion stood, jaw dropping in shock, muscles tense as if ready to spring into action. He froze, awaiting his brother's response.

Zariah's eyes wildly spun from silver to gold and back again, around and around as he visibly worked to control himself and his inner dragon.

My eyes narrowed and I ignored the sting in my hand, daring him to deny what he'd done or act in any way indignant.

A growl erupted from his throat and Zion jerked forward, but I put up my hand and kept my nasty look pinned on Zariah. Zion halted, his hands twitching as he held himself back.

Funny how he was the one with the most control of his human self, but not his dragon. Zariah was the opposite. If his dragon *and* human selves wanted to fight, we'd dance. I'd been in enough scraps in the mud quarter that I wasn't afraid of him.

"You got something to say?" I spit at Zariah.

"She's injured. You're being an asshole. Apologize," Zion said to his brother.

Zariah's attention shifted to his brother, golden eyes large and challenging.

"You made her cry, from what you told me. You disparaged her people, our father, and yourself, you nitwit."

Zion shot me a nervous look, then focused again on Zariah. Then it clicked: he was trying to shift Zariah's anger onto him to protect me.

My ire deflated in an instant, my shoulders drooping as I leaned back against a hard, cold stone wall. With everything that had happened, how could I linger on a stupid fight? Yeah it hurt, but only because Zion and Zariah mattered to me. No one else in the mud quarter had, besides my mother and Shava.

Maybe I could settle with just being supremely annoyed at him, and demanding an apology. I winced as sudden pain overtook my body, likely held back by my adrenaline rush at waking up.

Zion pushed his brother down into the ground and was at my side a moment later. Zariah shook his head and the gold in his eyes cleared instantly. He moved behind me, his hand stroking soothing circles on my back. Actions spoke louder than words.

"Easy there. The injury is on the inside, so we

couldn't really heal you while you were unconscious. Drink this though."

Oh. I was injured. That made sense. Zariah frowned and pulled out a small vial with a dark blue substance in it. It was then I noticed the bruises and cuts littering his face, and that one of his arms was in a makeshift split. He looked like hell.

My annoyance shifted into concern. He'd taken enough licks. He didn't need any more from me.

"I'm sorry, flower," he whispered into my ear. "I'm a horrid beast. Not all of these bruises are from my mother."

His eyes darted to Zion, whose eyes flashed gold for just a fraction of a second before the silver was back, his concerned gaze on me.

Zion had attacked Zariah on my behalf?

I almost laughed. Almost.

"I could have pummeled him. I'm the better fighter. But I deserved it." Zariah nipped at my ear, his face dotted with black, blue, and yellow bruises. "I won't heal them. I need the reminder. I need you to know I'm sorry. It won't happen again."

Tears gathered again in my eyes, but for a different reason this time. I blinked them away, not sure what to do with the rising emotions in my chest. We didn't have time for forgiveness and absolution in the mud quarter.

"What's in the bottle?" I questioned instead, eager to change the subject.

"Poison," he bit back immediately, a grin stretching his mouth and laughter in his eyes, despite the lingering exhaustion. Not amused, I snatched the vial and downed it in one go.

And nearly retched it back up.

Zion patted my back like I was a baby.

"Oh no, you don't," Zariah chimed in helpfully. "Keep it down. There's more if you don't, though."

I fought the nausea for what felt like an excruciatingly long time, but was likely only a few seconds. Soon enough it cleared, and I could breathe again. The pain in my side dissipated, and I cautiously stood.

"Let's debrief," Zariah declared, grabbing my arm and leading me toward a cave. Dully, I realized we were on the same cliff we'd been before, and the same cave with supplies and a small fire.

"Zariah, give her a moment for the sake of the gods. She just—"

"She's a big girl who will want to know what's going on immediately," Zariah countered.

Zion's pupils dilated and flashed gold as he snarled. Zariah shoved me behind him and squared off against his brother, muscles taut.

"Absolutely fucking not," I yelled at both of them, pushing Zariah's arm away and stepping in between them. "I've had enough shit for one day, quit adding to the pile!"

Both of them shrunk inwardly at my words, moodily glaring at each other but mutely following me inside of the cave.

We sat down around the fire and stared into the flames for a few moments.

"I'm sorry I left like that," I directed at them. "Surely you know I wasn't actually leaving," I began, wanting to get that clear before anything else. I shifted uncomfortably, frowning as there was no pain at all to be found, when minutes ago it'd wracked my body.

There was a lingering awkwardness between us still from the angry words and suspicions from the last time we'd met.

"What was that stuff you gave me?" I said instead, wincing at the not-so-subtle change in topic. Was it something available only to the princes, or anyone on the Seat?

Zariah shot Zion a look. Zion put a hand over his head, not quite meeting my eyes. "Well, Zion told me about that one time he uh ... licked you, and we started experimenting."

"It was our blood. Our blood has healing properties," Zariah burst in, unable to contain his enthusiasm. "Neat, isn't it?"

I blinked slowly. "I just drank ... your blood?!"

"Our dragon's blood, technically," Zariah piped cheerfully at the look of horror on my face. "Oh, cheer up. We were thinking maybe we could try it on the sick Nobles. That is—"

His face went slack, a blush creeping up his cheeks as he went silent.

I had a few guesses.

"Yeah, I heard. I get it now, though. You having to obey the queen is some sort of weird dragon hierarchy thing, isn't it?"

Both boys' shoulders loosened with relief. "Something like that," Zion confirmed while Zariah grumpily kicked an ember that had rolled out of the fire.

Fire.

I stood up fast and shot toward the cave opening, intending on looking back toward the kingdom where I knew the mud quarter was. Or had been.

I didn't get that far.

Down below me were dozens of campfires—like stars that had fallen from the heavens and lit the harsh, unforgiving landscape with their glow. How long had I been out? The entire day? Two days?

"Are they—"

"Zariah and I worked together with Zephyr to get the survivors out. Zariah kept the queen distracted while I ushered out as many as I could. Zephyr is down there now, seeing to them. You've been out a day and a half."

I whipped around to face them, emotion tightening my throat. "Is that how you got injured?" I managed to Zariah, my voice wobbling.

"Technically, though it's his fault he couldn't see through the smoke and flew face first into a wall," Zion supplied helpfully, smirking at his brother.

I didn't listen any further. I ran and leaped at Zariah, wrapping my arms around him and seizing his lips with mine.

His muscles tightened then relaxed around me as he eagerly devoured me, both of us lost in the kiss as teeth scraped and fingers grasped.

Zion huffed behind us, but I paid him no mind.

My fingernails raked through Zariah's hair, a small growl rumbling from his chest he held me tightly to him. He turned and slammed my back up against the cave wall, the pressure delicious as I felt him rub and push against me.

"She *just* healed! Aren't you being a bit—"

Zion cut himself off as Zariah left my lips and attacked my neck and collarbone, his dragon fangs pushing from his gums and leaving a fiery trail as he bit and nipped. I caught Zion's eye over Zariah's shoulder, watching the uncontrollable shift from silver to gold with fascination. Every muscle in his body looked taut, as though he were about to explode.

And yet he stayed, allowing Zariah and I our moment.

I reached a hand out to him over Zariah's shoulder, and he came toward me like a puppet called by its master.

I pulled Zion beside me and kissed him.

"Get behind her," he growled at Zion, and soon I was surrounded on both sides by warmth.

"Hold her."

Zion's arms went underneath my armpits as Zariah went low, his large hands pinning my hips against Zion. I hooked my arms around Zion's neck and held on for dear life.

More secure, Zion let one hand drift down and underneath my tunic, gently skimming one hand over a nipple as I shuddered against him. Zariah had my pants off two seconds later, leaving me bare to the cold air.

With one heave, Zariah was on his knees before me, lifting me up and setting me down on his shoulders. Zion leaned me back so I faced the cave ceiling, and Zariah stuck his nose into my core and licked.

Zion bent down and claimed my mouth, muffling my groans and cries as Zariah nipped and sucked. Zion's hand on my breast grew more forceful, pinching and rolling my nipple as his fangs descended into my mouth. Boldly, I wrapped my tongue around one, and felt him nearly drop me.

"Zephyr said you injured him. Naughty girl,

breaking his ribs like that. Even if he is our half-brother."

My eyes rolled back into my head as Zariah added his fingers, spreading me open before him and rubbing maddening circles with one hand while thrusting in and out with the other. And all the while his tongue kept swirling and stroking ...

"He's ... kinda ... a dick. He's fine, isn't he?" I choked out, my thoughts as scrambled as the dirt mash my mother used to make when we ran out of real food.

Zariah's grip tightened painfully as he wrapped his hand around my hip bones. His face glistened with moisture, wet from *me*.

"Talking about another man while we're working our wings off here? That's just as naughty."

He picked me up and carried me past the fire and into the corner of the cave where a few old, discarded furs were scattered. Zariah gestured to Zion to lay down first. "Go ahead, it's your turn. Though not yet. She needs to ask forgiveness for asking after another man while my tongue was inside her."

I knew he was teasing from the grin on his face, but there was an animalistic frenzy in his eyes as well: one that let me know he was barely holding his dragon in check. I wondered what it would be like if both of them fully unleashed themselves on me.

"Jealous?" I goaded, rolling over onto my stomach just to be difficult. I heard Zariah growl from behind me as Zion sat down next to me.

"Oompf!"

I wasn't prepared as Zariah put an arm around my neck and buried his free hand in my hair, and yanked backwards.

"What was that, flower?"

The burn in my scalp and the pressure against my throat was delicious, but I wasn't about to let him know that. I wriggled my bum against his pelvis, arching my back naturally.

"Suck my brother's dick. That's a better use for your mouth, at the moment."

Zion's eyes went hooded as he freed himself from his pants and sat up in front of me, leaning back on his arms. Zariah kept me held tightly in his grasp, pushing me into Zion's lap.

"Go on. Suck him."

Yessir, I thought, opening my mouth and taking Zion in one go. Zariah let go of my hair as Zion took over, fingers digging into my scalp as every muscle into his body went rigid.

"That's a good girl. Suck him long and hard."

Oh, I'm gonna.

I moved slowly and methodically up and down Zion's shaft, hollowing my cheeks using my tongue to run across his tip. A sound that was half-human, half-dragon escaped Zion's throat, his eyes gold and feral as he watched my mouth slide over his cock. Zariah shifted his grip so one hand held both of my wrists behind my back. The other smoothed itself up and down my back.

"That's it. He likes that, doesn't he?"

I don't know what it was about being held down and forced to do something I'd happily do anyway, but combined with Zariah's dirty talk, I was quickly losing my mind. I went faster on Zion, who hissed in between his teeth and started pushing and pulling my head where he wanted it.

"That's it. Let's see if we can't make him lose control, eh?"

Sounded good to me. I wanted it rough. I wanted it hard.

I sucked and moaned against Zion's cock, and he made a choked sound before snapping entirely, roughly grabbing my head and shoving it down on his dick as he fucked my mouth hard and fast.

It was uncomfortable and messy, but I loved it. I loved the loss of control. I loved the feel of his swollen cock as it stretched my mouth and went down the back of my throat, spittle running down my chin and onto his lap.

Without warning, Zariah grabbed me by the throat and chest and yanked me back, Zion's cock coming out of my mouth with a loud pop. Zion snarled and leaped at me, but Zariah pushed him down.

"Get control or you're not coming near her," Zariah threatened, fangs pushing through his gums as he snarled at his brother.

Zion's face twisted, but his eyes flicked from gold to silver and back again a few times, before fading to his familiar silver tinged with green.

"All right?" Zariah asked cautiously, still keeping me clutched against him.

Zion blinked at me with mild horror. "Fine. Are you—"

"Loved it," I deadpanned, not having any patience for regret or hesitation.

"All right. Let's keep going," Zariah ordered. "Lie back down."

Zion's eyes narrowed but he complied, lying down on his back but staying propped up on his elbows.

Zariah glared back at the small bit of defiance, but shook it off.

"How about you ride the dragon, flower?" Zariah nipped playfully at the back of my neck. I arched against him automatically, practically purring. He gently pushed me down toward his brother and I complied, pouting a bit.

Zion's cock was already at attention for me. I crawled into his lap and straddled him, lining up my hips until he was poised at my entrance. I hesitated, wanting to be just a little difficult.

"Mari," Zariah grumbled at my back.

I shot him a grin over my shoulder as Zion's hands formed an iron grip on my hip bones and shoved me down on his cock.

I gasped at the sudden intrusion, but the fullness and warmth of him quickly spread through my entire body.

"Yes, that's it. Now ride him."

Zion and I moved against each other as Zariah went behind me, running his hands over my body. It was so much sensation that I moaned.

"You hear that? Such an eager little flower."

"I'm gonna 'flower' you if you don't cut it out," I gasped out.

Zariah chuckled as his hand snuck up my throat. "Is that so? *Flower?*"

I growled and tried to throw him off, but he held me too tightly. Secretly, I was thrilled at the dominance and struggle play. It was a safe way of testing my boundaries and limits. And so, so hot.

Zion bucked beneath me, snapping his hips and grinding against me, his grip so hard I knew he would leave bruises on my hips. The thought only turned me on more.

"Do you want both dragons at the same time?" Zariah breathed into my ear. I trembled a bit at thought, willing but also unsure and cautious.

"What—"

"Just relax. Do you trust us not to hurt you?"

His hand flexed over my throat, squeezing and loosening reflexively. I made a hum of satisfaction.

"I like being hurt a bit," I protested. I wasn't some fragile flower like Freesia or the twins. I was a survivor. I was a mud girl.

Zariah's nose nuzzled into the middle of my shoulder blade as he inhaled my scent. "Just relax."

Gently, he pushed me down so I was chest to chest with Zion, who enthusiastically seized the opportunity to pull one of my breasts into his mouth. My hips moved faster as he sucked and bit on the nipple, my distraction so great I barely noticed as Zariah got into position behind me, one hand splayed on my lower back. He reached down with one hand and covered it in my juices, then withdrew, sending a new wave of heat between my legs.

"Relax."

His cock nudged up against my rear, and pushed in carefully. I tensed immediately out of reflex. Zion grabbed my hair and bit down hard on my breast. I went boneless and cried out in pleasure, and Zariah pushed forward. It stung, but only a little. It also felt ... full, and dangerously right.

I bucked back against Zariah, and he sank a little further. He hissed in surprise, and Zion tugged me back down, demanding my attention as he gave a hard thrust up into me.

"Easy. We need to share. Give and take, so we don't hurt her." Zariah lectured Zion.

I expected Zion to snap at his brother like he had all night with his possessive dragon, but he only nodded solemnly. My worries vanished; both of my dragons were in control and focused on me.

Zariah pushed again, groaning in appreciation as he sat fully seated in me as I relaxed. My breathing hitched as he ran a hand up and down my back in a soothing circle. "Good girl. Such a good girl. Isn't she, Zion?"

Zion didn't answer, still in the middle of his feast on my breasts. Zariah took the opportunity to thrust a few times, then went still. Zion thrust up next, and soon both of them established a rhythm that had my mind wiped blank of any thoughts. It was only me, them, and the sensation of being so utterly complete I could have died content.

"Gods, she's incredible," Zariah grit against my ear. Zion made a strangled noise of agreement, but I wasn't focused on them anymore. My own release was building, especially as Zariah bent over me, his fingers slipping down to rub and tease. I bucked and writhed against him, desperately trying to scratch an itch that kept evading me.

"Don't tense. Just let it happen," he soothed. "Take both of our cocks. Take them."

My mind ceased to work as I let go of all my inhibitions and gave myself up fully to them. That elusive itch in my core stretched higher and higher, and I realized I'd never be able to stay angry at either of them over anything. They were my world, and I was theirs.

I was close to falling over the edge, feeling the brink so sharply I stopped breathing. A sting on my neck pulled me back, the pain keeping from teething over the edge at the last second. A whine of protest escaped my throat even as I dully registered that Zion had sunk two fangs into my neck. My entire body went limp and warm. It was like liquid pleasure was replacing every last drop of blood. I waited for Zariah to get angry or chastise Zion for letting his dragon take control once again, but he was silent.

And then another sharp pain exploded across the back of my neck as Zariah sank his fangs into the back of my throat. My gasp of surprise morphed into a throaty moan. Wildly I tried to grind my hips into both of them, but they held me absolutely still as they drank from me, four hands holding me in place by my neck, arms, and waist.

I didn't know what was happening, but I didn't care. I could wander through one thousand kingdoms and not snatch a single moment as glorious as this. Every secret of every mystery could have bared themselves before me, and I would have shut my eyes and shoved them away in favor of this perfect, blissful moment.

"Take us as we take you," Zariah growled from behind me, his voice reverberating in my chest and through my blood as he was still embedded in my flesh in more ways than one. Zion released me from the front, but before I could protest, he bit down again with his fangs, right into my breast.

I cried out, my fingers digging harshly into his hair

and twisting. Hot blood ran down my neck since Zariah hadn't closed the wound, but I didn't care. It felt right. This was dark. This was dirty.

This was everything.

I exploded into millions of tiny pieces, just like the glittering stars that twinkled overhead.

CHAPTER NINE

It was blissful sleep, but the moment my eyes shot open, the full horror of everything I'd witnessed slammed into me. I bolted upwards, the arms around me dropping away.

"I need to get down there! What if the queen comes back? They're just out in the open and exposed and in danger of—"

Zion put a hand gently on my mouth, dragging me back into his arms. "Mother won't be coming back. Her dragon is a secret she holds closely to her chest—We didn't even know until yesterday. She'll be pissed she didn't kill everyone, but you don't have to worry about her swooping in to finish the job. The final ball that marks the end of the reaping is tomorrow night, so she'll be kept busy with that." He paused, frowning. "Though I agree, we need to move these people somewhere safe. I was waiting until you woke up to take you down to talk to Zephyr."

I flinched at the mention of the half-brother who'd tried to murder me. Seemed a theme with family members.

"Oh. Uh ... all right."

I'd be damned if I let my people bunker down with dangerous demons and Zephyr, who didn't seem to give a shit about any of the danger.

"Plus, Zariah is out patrolling. He's been trying to show them he's being protective, but ... uh, they haven't exactly been receptive. Zephyr is going nuts trying to keep everyone from bolting. We need you to help with this." Zion's eyes went unfocused for a moment, a telltale sign he was communicating with his brother.

His gaze sharpened again on me. "Right. Incoming."

Before I could open my mouth, heat and gold scales filled the mouth of the cave. Zariah shuffled in awkwardly with his large dragon body, tucking his wings into his back.

"You and I are going to ride Zariah down to the survivors, and reassure them that the gold dragon is meant to protect them. We don't want to be a symbol of fear any longer. At least not to everyone."

His face tightened at that in sorrow, and I couldn't blame him.

I brushed the dirt and soot from my clothes as best I could, and touched my hair to see how bad it was. Oh well, there was nothing for it, was there?

I sighed. "Let's go."

Zariah bent his long neck down, and I climbed up using his neck spikes. Zion watched me carefully, then repeated my steps as best he could, settling behind me. I eyed his boots as he carefully tucked them up and away from Zariah's wing joints.

Ready?

I nodded, then realized the question hadn't come from Zion's voice behind me. Zariah's inflection was in my head, reverberating and echoing deeply like it never had out loud.

Exhaustion was getting the better of me. That was the logical explanation.

Carefully, Zariah backed out of the cave and did a smart little turn so that we faced the cliff. In the morning light, the small refugee camp looked pitiful, and they were pointing at us and crying out in fear.

Just get it over with. Zariah's voice came again in my head. Before I could remark on it, Zion cut over me.

"Agreed," he murmured in my ear.

With a mighty leap, Zariah leaped into the air, wings spread wide. There was that usual momentary feeling of utter weightlessness—that second of terror when I was convinced we would plummet to our deaths. His wings beat furiously on either side of me, and we leveled out into a smooth glide.

The descent was quick, and Zariah slammed heavily to the ground on his clawed feet. The screams of terror broke my heart, but they, at least, weren't running at seeing me and Prince Zion perched atop the dragon's back, unharmed and alive. That, or they were simply too curious to help themselves.

I slid down Zariah's back too quickly, my arms out in a plea for them to understand. "No! It's all right! The gold dragon is here to protect you! He chased away the dragon that hurt you—the silver one! Do you remember?"

Confused faces stared back at me until understanding dawned.

"It *was* a silver dragon.... I knew it looked different!" breathed one girl behind me, her eyes wide with shock.

Zephyr pushed himself forward, wincing as he limped forward. Shava was right behind him, pinning me with a glare. Something inside of me broke a little.

The bastard prince and I locked gazes, then glanced away.

I have something that might help.

Before I could respond, Zariah's huge wings unfurled, and he took off into the air. I wanted desperately to ask Zion about what I was hearing, but he took that moment to step forward, his arms outstretched toward the refugees.

"Do not be afraid of the gold dragon. I am here, and the dragon tamer walks among you. Sleep easily and rest after your ordeal. We will make plans to move you somewhere safer soon."

He gave everyone a winning smile.

Whumpf.

There were a few shrieks and squeals as huge chunks of meat hit the dirt, dropped over by Zariah. The golden dragon wheeled around in the sky and landed on the outskirts of the crowd, walking forward and putting his head down to nudge my hand.

The people eyed the charred carcasses with hunger and a bit of caution.

"Go ahead," Zion encouraged them. "The dragon wishes to provide for you."

Zephyr and Shava stepped forward, taking charge and separating people into groups to skin and gut the meat, tasking others with collecting sticks for spits.

Energized with purpose and the promise of a hot meal, the crowd dispersed in a flurry of activity, leaving Zariah's golden frame, Zion, Zephyr, and Shava.

The bastard prince kept shooting worried glances at me. Shava looked ready to burst. I had to act first if I had any shot of keeping this from exploding in our faces, or anyone getting barbequed. Zephyr and I's last meeting hung in the air between us like a rancid scent.

"Thank you for looking after my people," I told Zephyr sincerely, my voice wavering a bit. He blinked, clearly not expecting that. Was he a sick bastard? Yes. Did some shriveled part of his heart actually think he was doing the right thing? Unfortunately, also yes.

"Oh. Um ... of course. I brought the others out from the tunnels to join them," he mumbled, gaze going to the ground.

I bit back a small smile, realizing he'd taken my advice about separating the turning Nobles from those who'd fled the Seat. He just didn't want to admit to it.

"You're just going to forget what she did?" Shava snapped at him.

Zariah growled at her sudden aggression, and Zephyr put himself between the massive dragon and Shava.

"Mari did what she felt was best. I was doing what I thought was best. We're *all* trying our best," Zephyr emphasized diplomatically.

Perhaps he was the one who should have been the heir, I thought wryly.

"But speaking of doing our best," Zephyr continued, "Mari helped me realize the situation underground with the changing Nobles in untenable conditions."

Untenable? What did that mean?

I tried to give Shava a pleading look, but her arms were crossed over her chest and she was steadfastly ignoring me. It would have hurt less if she'd been the one trying to kill me.

"What do you suggest?" Zion asked coolly.

It was odd seeing all three men (well, two men and a dragon) going toe-to-toe. Zephyr looked so similar to them yet more rugged and unyielding since his face and frame held none of the queen's delicate features.

"I suggest that I lead the refugees away from here. We can cross the desert together, and find a new land to settle on. Let the queen have her corrupted, demonic court."

Zion's brow furrowed in thought.

And how is that supposed to work, exactly? boomed Zariah's voice in my head. **Wrap this up. I want to take Mari back to the cliff and—**

That was it. I wasn't ignoring it anymore. I whipped around and cuffed him lightly on the nose. "How about you get your mind out of the gutter and actually contribute?"

The golden dragon's jaw dropped, incredulous. It was so comical I almost laughed. Zion whipped around and stared.

"You can—"

"Hear your little telepathic nonsense now? Yeah. Lucky me," I grumbled, rolling my eyes.

Zephyr's head tilted to the side, intrigued. "I've

read quite a bit about dragons. I thought the section about telepathy between mates had been exaggerated, though." He smirked. "So you all *have* mated."

The word was strange to my ears. "Mates?" I asked.

Zariah rumbled with satisfaction behind me, nuzzling his snout into my bum. I slammed my palm into his nose again, but this time with force. He whined, but withdrew.

Zephyr raised an eyebrow. "Dragons are magickal creatures, created from wild magick and will that manifests itself. In your cause, the witch who cursed the queen and you. Dragons only have one mate throughout their lifetime. This is a destined mate that could be anywhere in the world. Dragons who don't find their mate go insane, or die." He frowned. "The rules on procreating are unclear." He gave Zion and Zariah a tilt of his head.

I tried to take all of that in. "Procreate?" I said instead, latching onto the one concrete thing I could grasp.

Zariah huffed with amusement. **He means hopefully there won't be any little dragon babies cooking in there.**

His head nudged my belly gently.

My lips parted in shock. *Baby dragons?* Thank the gods.

"The queen had the princes, though," I argued, still confused.

Zephyr shrugged his shoulders. "I don't know all of the rules, obviously. Maybe there's more nuances to the curse. Maybe the queen was pregnant when she was cursed. Maybe the curse specifically attaches to her bloodline. It's hard to say."

So really, he didn't know much at all. My disappointment must have shown, because Zion put an arm around my shoulders.

"What can you tell us, then?" he asked patiently.

Zephyr sighed. "Just bits and pieces. It's important for dragons to find their mates. Seems you're all right in that regard." He nodded toward me, and I flushed.

"But otherwise there wasn't much. Just that you're made of magick, the change is permanent, and try not to burn down the countryside."

"The power to turn into a dragon doesn't seem like much of a curse," I said, snorting a bit. "Seems right up your mother's alley, anyway."

My boys had nothing to say to that, and the awkward tension grew.

"Back to leading the refugees to another land," Zion pivoted, his voice serious. "We have flown over the desert. To reach another kingdom will be a long and dangerous road, and you can't be sure of your welcome. What if you're all killed on sight?"

Zephyr's eyes flared with challenge. "They wouldn't dare if we had a dragon with us."

Everyone tensed. Even Zariah. I put a hand on his snout, urging him to keep control. It wasn't him I needed to worry about, though. Zion looked ready to spit fire himself.

"If you're suggesting either of us leave Mari—"

"She could come too. I assumed she'd want to be with her people," Zephyr insisted, his nose sticking a bit in the air.

Zion turned to me. "Well? What do you think?"

What? This was on me? "You'd leave your kingdom?" I clarified, unable to believe it.

Zion grabbed my hands in his. "We'd do anything for you, Mari."

Zephyr smirked. "Mates," he whispered dramatically to Shava, whose lip curled in disdain. He unconsciously rubbed the spot on his wrist where I knew his skin was changing to ash, but his long sleeves covered it for now. He caught me staring and blanched, all the color draining from his face.

My mouth opened to argue, realizing there was no way he could join the refugees. Not when he could turn at a moment's notice.

"Zephyr can't lead. He—"

I stopped myself at the ashen look on the bastard prince's face. He was bat-shit crazy, but he meant well. He was trying to help in his own fucked up way. I should tell Zariah and Zion he was just as infected as the other Nobles and would eventually turn. What did it matter though? As long as I watched him, we could ensure he didn't hurt anyone. Shouldn't Zephyr be allowed to live his life as much as he could before the inevitable end, just like he allowed the other doomed Nobles?

If it came down to it, a dragon would be more than enough to deal with one rogue demon.

I cleared my throat. "I mean ... the mud quarter people don't know you. But obviously that will change," I ended lamely. "What about the demons and the Nobles? Who will ... help them?"

Help being an odd word to use for what Zephyr did, but still a good question.

Zephyr shifted his weight restlessly, eyes shifting to Zion. "I don't know how much they told you about what the queen did. When the dragon—er, Zariah, put himself between the refugees and her, she went straight for the tunnels and doused them in dragonfire. I don't—I assume ... That is, they all have to be dead, don't they?"

A pit of dread opened in my stomach. "What ... What about the new Nobles who turn? Where will they go?"

Zephyr wouldn't look at me. Zion had turned away, and even Zariah's dragon head stared off in the distance.

"But ... I thought that was your mission," I protested to Zephyr. "How can you, of all people, write off the turning Nobles?"

There was no way he could miss the sharpness of my voice, but Zephyr grit his teeth and said nothing. It was a silent change. Would I call his bluff?

I finally looked away. I couldn't condemn Zephyr, and if the queen had already decimated the demons in the pit, there wasn't anything that could be done now, could there?

Zephyr clapped his hands together, enthusiastic now that he knew I wasn't going to spill his secret. "Well, the animals should be about skinned. What say the dragon help get the fire going?"

I'm interested in other fires.... Zariah grumbled, but as my eyes narrowed at him, he blew a puff of hot air out of his snout and trotted behind Zephyr deeper into the camp.

Pig, I thought back, directing it at his large dragon behind. He paused in shock, head whipping around to stare at me before turning back to shuffle after Zephyr like an overly large dog.

Zion squeezed my shoulder. "You probably just turned him on more."

I gestured helplessly. "Breathing turns him on."

The smell of barbeque filled the air.

CHAPTER
TEN

With Zariah's help (in dragon form, of course), we all built a blazing bonfire in the center of the little camp. This led to a strange, festive air that didn't sit right with the smoldering ruins of the mud quarter back in the city.

But I also knew people from the mud quarter had never had a reason to celebrate before. Or hot meat. Or a giant, golden symbol of protection and redemption that was a literal light in the darkness that was our existence.

Then again, I would have been thrilled to get out of the mud quarter. I hadn't been attached to anyone other than my mother, my few friends already gone and taken to the Seat. Looking back wasn't a mud quarter trait; looking back didn't do you any good.

So in a way, I understood the happy, nearly crazed atmosphere. With their lighter hair, the surviving women and children from the Seat stuck out like sore thumbs, but they sat side by side with refugees from the mud quarter. The children ate the meat with wide, astonished eyes, one child crying in happiness when Zion offered him seconds.

It was too much. The suffering here compared to life on the Seat was so jarring that I wanted to scream at the injustice.

"Here. Don't think I forgot about you."

Zion handed me a giant drumstick. I grasped the greasy meat in my fingers, frowning at it.

"Where did Zariah get this? The land around here ..."

The tips of Zion's ears blushed red. "It's ... Well, there are kingdoms far from here that aren't so far for a dragon. And their farms are large, with huge herds of prey—I mean, animals. Trust me, they won't miss these."

I wasn't sure how I felt about stealing meat from others, but you couldn't argue that the people here didn't need it. I hoped that in time, the sickly, gaunt look of most of the children and women would fade. It hadn't escaped me that almost no men had made it out of the mud quarter; not that there had been many there to begin with. Whether it was by chance or design, I didn't want to know. These women, at least, deserved a space to feel safe without having to look over their shoulders constantly. I made a mental note to speak to Zephyr about it later. He'd have to keep a sharp eye on the men, who were used to taking whatever they wanted.

"Sit and eat. Everyone else has. It's your turn." Zion guided me down in front of the fire, next to Zephyr and Shava. Zephyr gave me a small grin but Shava ignored me. It hurt, but I couldn't force her to do anything she didn't want to.

I ate slowly, reveling in the companionable silence as we all kept to ourselves. The crackling of the fire was soothing, as well as the muted voices of the refugees in the background, happy and excited and feeling safe for the first time in their lives.

I couldn't ruin the atmosphere by revealing Zephyr's ashy little problem, could I? Zion was smiling as he chatted to his half-brother. Zariah was down on all fours as children cautiously approached him; they then shrieked with delight as they raced each other to climb up his back and neck spikes and be declared 'king of the dragon.'

Everyone was happy except for me.

My thoughts kept drifting back to the queen. I was on edge and anxious despite what Zion had said. I was sure the queen would be occupied with a ball tonight, but they were fools if they thought she'd forgotten about us.

"Don't you have to go to the ball?" I asked Zion. Zariah's large dragon head swerved to face me.

Zion blinked. "You honestly think we'd do anything for her after what she'd done for you?"

A small, giddy thrill went through me, but I pushed it down just for the moment. "So she didn't order you to attend the ball?"

Zariah growled. **Mother assumes we will do a lot of things. She's only recently beginning to realize she will have to get more specific with her orders.**

That didn't sit well with me. "What could it hurt to just go and maintain the illusion you're still obedient in most things? You could scout out what people are saying, and—"

We aren't going, Mari, Zariah insisted.

Zion nodded. "Fuck her."

It made my heart lift, but the ascent was tempered a bit by the sinking sensation in my stomach. I shook my head, catching Zephyr glaring at both of his brothers. My eyes narrowed.

"Do you know I've read books about witches?" I jerked as Zephyr scooted closer to me, Shava busy helping a mother with a baby and Zion and Zariah playing with the children.

"Witches?" I asked dully, not really interested.

"Yes, like the one that laid this curse. They come in different kinds, I guess. Each represents an element like air, water, fire, that sort of thing."

I stared at the remaining meat in my hands and ate it just to give myself something to do other than talk to Zephyr.

"It's fascinating," he continued, his enthusiasm not in the least bit dampened by my aloofness. "There's also different kinds of magick: black and white."

That was interesting, I supposed. "Like good and evil?"

Zephyr scoffed. "No, not at all. Different kinds of energies. Good and evil is subjective, anyway. Did you think mercy killing the demons was evil, or a 'good' thing to do?"

I squirmed under his intense stare, but he quickly moved on. "My point is, they're just different types of energy. The books say magickal creatures can harness both, but it's horrendously difficult. Most pick one or the other. Neat, eh?"

I guess. It didn't really affect me because I wasn't a magickal creature, was I?

Zephyr drew back, hands flexing on his knees. "I thought you'd be more interested."

My shoulders shrugged. "There aren't any witches around here, are there?"

He gave me a morose look, and I sighed. I should at least try to get along with him, shouldn't I? "Well, what kind of witch do you think laid the curse?"

He perked up immediately. "Ah, now that is a worthy question. It's hard to say. Cursing a bloodline to be dragons hardly fits a particular element, does it?"

"Maybe fire," I suggested half-heartedly, tossing the remnants of my bone into the large fire. It sizzled where it hit the flames, the last scraps of meat and juices hissing and burning up.

Zephyr and I descended into silence: his thoughtful and mine agitated. I couldn't keep it pushed down any longer.

"Zephyr," I began quietly, so as not to attract anyone else's attention, "while I appreciate you volunteering to lead the refugees to a better home, you know you can't do that. What about the ..." I gestured vaguely to his sleeves, under which I knew his demon transformation was already beginning.

I thought he'd get scared again, or even angry. Instead, at the mention of his little condition, Zephyr smiled widely. "Ah, Mari, don't worry about that. I've found a solution!"

My lips parted in shock. "To stop the change?" I asked out loud, remembering how vehemently he'd protested the possibility—right before I'd almost crushed him to death.

Accidentally.

Zephyr drew a long draught from his canteen, smacking his lips and wiping them with the back of his sleeve, all the while grinning broadly. "I have you to thank, really. You said 'we don't have magick.' Do you remember?"

I didn't, but I'd tried to block most of that last meeting from my memories.

"Anyway, you were half right. Humans don't have magick. But those with Noble blood do, you see? The witch gifted it to us along with the curse. We can't change into demons without some kind of magick in our veins, can we? I'm so thankful to you for this realization, I am willing to drop our little feud and lead your little muddies to freedom."

I nodded slightly, just to appease his sudden zeal. Had he just called my people 'muddies?'

"Well, as I lay there hoping I wasn't bleeding internally, I realized that if I had magick, maybe I could try some of the white and black rituals written down in the book. So you see, our little squabble was necessary for the greater picture."

The fervent gleam in his eyes wasn't encouraging.

"And did you try any rituals?" I asked cautiously.

He scoffed, leaning back on his log and crossing his arms over his chest. The tension broke as easily as snapping a twig. "Well, no. There's a lot you need to do for a ritual. I will, though."

"And this ... ritual ... will keep you from changing?" I clarified.

He only grinned, gave me a patronizing pat on the head, and walked off.

Well, at least he wasn't trying to kill me anymore.

And anything that helped my people was a good thing ... right?

I was spared any more hard thinking as Shava stomped over to and sat down in Zephyr's recently vacated spot. She glared over my shoulder and I turned, seeing him give her an emphatic gesture. Shava rolled her eyes before she stared at the ground.

"Zephyr is making me talk to you. I don't want to," she grit out. "Said something about it being my last chance to settle things. Don't know what the hell he's on about."

"That's obvious," I shot back. A sigh escaped me, my hand running through my dry hair. "Shava, what happened to us? We were best friends. You were like a mother to me." *Everything was fine before you made your entire personality about Zephyr.*

I stopped before saying that, knowing that if I brought him into it we'd never get anywhere.

"You nearly killed him, Mari. What if I'd hurt one of your little dragon princes like that?"

My mouth opened to argue, but I shut it. She was right; I'd be beyond pissed.

"Well, those little dragon princes also healed him. And he's fine, and not even mad about it," I countered. If only she knew about what he was doing, and how he tortured people! She wouldn't be so willing to stick up for him!

"I can't wait until we finally leave this place," Shava growled, kicking a bit of sand with her boots. "If you come with us, just stay away from me." She stalked away, and my shoulders drooped.

I should tell her. I could tell her and watch the smug look on her face fade away to horror and shock.

But I couldn't. I owed my early and then continued survival in the mud quarter to Shava. I'd honor that by keeping my mouth shut, even if it meant she continued living in a delusion, strutting around like a peacock. At least she was happy.

What a lovely evening.

It was surreal to be sitting in front of the fire, surrounded by smiling, happy faces yet alone. I relished the opportunity to have my own thoughts, but I felt so detached from everything going on around me. It was just like the ball—surrounded by hundreds of people who had no sense of what was truly going on.

Heather and Hyacinthe. Azalea and Leilani. Even Freesia.

I didn't know what plans we had exactly, but I couldn't leave the kingdom until I knew my friends were safe. I wanted to give them the choice to stay or go. That meant going back to the palace, whether I liked it or not. I wasn't afraid of the queen—I was afraid of what she could do to my mother, my father, and possibly my brother.

My jaw cracked as I yawned, bringing Zion to my side instantly.

You can go to sleep, Zariah's voice rang in my head.

"Agreed. You've had a traumatic day." Zion put a hand on the small of my back.

I snorted. "No more traumatic than anything else that's happened since I was reaped."

Zion flinched at that, but I ignored it. It was true. Death trailed me wherever I went.

"I need to get my family out of the castle, or talk to them and give them a choice if they're coming with us or not when the refugees leave," I said instead, deflecting. Ell at least was somewhere he in the camp, but my mother and my brother were still up at the castle.

Zion frowned.

About that, Zariah added, gently shaking off the lasting laughing child and sauntering over in his massive dragon form.

I stood, panic racing through my veins. "You're staying here?" I shrieked, my voice much higher than it should have been. The people closest turned and stared, and I struggled to soften my tone.

"I mean, I guess I'm not surprised," I said wryly, hysterical laughter bubbling up in my throat. "You can't even rip a hangnail off without Mommy's permission. There's no way you could leave the kingdom."

I turned on my heel and left them both behind, picking and direction and just walking away from the camp. Once the bright light and warmth of the fire faded into the cold, harsh landscape of the blackened desert around me, I paused. Those stupid little buggy creatures would be out here. I couldn't even find an escape.

Growling in annoyance, I kicked a rock. The pain was sharp and biting, and exactly what I needed. Hot tears leaked from the corner of my eyes, but it felt good to just *feel* something.

A dragon soared overhead, perching on a high cliff and looking down on me.

You didn't let us finish, Zariah chided, tucking his head under one massive wing. **You know we can't leave because of our mother. So we need to stay and fight her. THEN we leave.**

You could have knocked me over with a feather. "You ... want to take down the queen?" My voice went high again. It was just unbelievable. Zariah and Zion were Momma's boys, bound to obey the queen. And here they were, plotting her downfall?

Zephyr told us about the etchings in the cave. It's only confirmed what we've suspected all along—this curse is her fault and our family's fault for enslaving your people. We want to make it right by setting them free. We may have to dethrone our mother to do that. We may have to kill her. But it's what's right. Isn't it? His voice broke on the last question, revealing how torn he was.

I focused my thoughts on him. **Come here.**

He swooped down from the cliff and landed roughly in front of me, the wind from his wings tossing the fringes of my hair around. I put my hand flat on his snout, the warmth of his body coursing through me.

Just make sure it's what you want to do for your kingdom and not what you think needs done for me, I cautioned him. What would challenging the queen even look like? We couldn't do it at the castle; she'd change into her dragon and hundreds would die! Worry clenched my gut thinking of my frail mother cowering before the queen's mighty silver dragon.

Nausea churned in my gut.

Be careful, I pleaded.

Zariah buried his snout in my neck, nuzzling me gently. The rough fraction of his scales against my skin felt soothing in an odd, visceral way.

A shadow fell over us and Zariah growled, but it was only Ell. I playfully shoved Zariah's nose away, standing. Awkwardness hung between as I blushed,

Ell's eyes taking me in as if he'd never really had a chance to before.

Which was true.

"I—" I began, only for him to shake his head at me. I fell silent, embarrassed. Hopefully he wasn't expecting some great declaration of love or something else ridiculous. Yes, he was my father, but he'd never been a true father. There was no anger; he'd done the best he could in the trapped situations we were all in, but we suddenly wouldn't have a strong relationship simply because he impregnated my mother.

"Just let me look at you," he said softly.

I crossed my arms over my chest, self-conscious. Zariah's massive figure next to me was reassuring, but I needed to face Ell on my own.

"There is a lot left unsaid. Everything you could think to say to me would be true. I deserve it," Ell began.

My mouth opened to protest, but I hesitated. He was right. He'd done a lot for my mother and me, but he'd hurt us as well.

"You're so strong. So beautiful. Just like her."

I jerked at that. "Who?"

"Your mother," Ell admitted sheepishly, staring at the ground. "I'm not proud of what happened. It caused her a lot of pain, but I'll never regret it because you're here. And we both wanted it at the time. We ... cared for each other, even if it didn't last. I wanted you to know that."

Emotion swelled in my chest, but I couldn't shake the image of the broken down woman that I associated with my mother.

"I don't think we're alike," I protested softly.

He cupped my cheek, lifting my eyes to meet his. Dark gazes connected, a world of pain shared uniquely in a way no one else would know but the two of us.

"You should have seen her twenty years ago, Mari. I fell in love the moment I saw her break another Fireguard's jaw for trying to put his hand under her skirt."

What?

I laughed, the sound bursting from me without warning at such an unimaginable scene. Ell chuckled and soon my arms were wrapped around him. He squeezed me so tightly to him that all the air escaped my lungs. I liked how it was too tight. It felt real.

Zariah breathed out through his nose behind me, and the moment was over. Ell's grip on me loosened, one hand softly patting the top of my head.

"Ok. Maybe we are alike," I admitted, wanting to believe it more than anything else in the world.

Ell sighed wistfully. "The mud quarter breaks people stronger than both of us. I knew you wouldn't let it break you. Never let anything break you."

I bit my lip and nodded. That I could promise.

Zariah growled from behind me, but I realized a second later that it wasn't because of Ell. Something was up. The hairs on my neck and arms stood on end, that uneasy feeling I'd felt in the cave sweeping over me.

"Is that ... " I began, only to break off as an odd noise stretched across the desert between our little camp and the kingdom.

What is that? I asked both him and Zion mentally. Zariah's dragon head tilted to the side as he listened hard.

It sounds like ... banging. I fell back as Zariah

growled and roared, jumping straight into the air and flapping his wings like mad.

I will investigate, he swore. **Get back to the others.**

My feet scraped harshly against the rough, blackened earth as I moved too quickly, nearly tripping and falling. My arms pumped as I ran back to the camp, dozens of different scenarios popping up in my head, and none of them good. Zion met me at the edge, lips set in a firm line.

They're ... banging at the wall, I think, came Zariah's voice. **The Fireguards have taken giant hammers and pickaxes, and they're striking it over and over again. I don't know—oh shit.**

A loud crack split the air, all activity in the camp stopping as everyone turned to look in the direction of the kingdom.

GATHER THE REFUGEES! RUN! THE QUEEN IS COMING WITH THE FIREGUARDS!

Oh no.

"RUN! GRAB WHAT YOU CAN AND RUN!" I screamed as loud as I could, racing past confused refugees. Where was Zephyr?! Where was Shava?

"THE QUEEN IS COMING WITH THE FIRE-GUARDS!" I tried again, being as clear and direct as possible. The noise in the distance grew louder as I recognized the sound of hundreds of pounding feet.

Zion raced toward me, then his brow set in a determined furrow. With a deep breath, he jumped and shifted mid-air, taking to the sky and circling around the refugees—hopefully buying them time.

"How did—" I cut myself off. There were better ways to communicate now other than shouting. **How** did you do that? I thought she forbade you from shifting together.

Zion's voice in my head was triumphant. **She only ever forbade us from patrolling the skies together. We always took it to mean we weren't to shift. Loopholes, darling.**

I grinned, but it was short lived as refugees streamed past me, tears in their eyes.

"How many Fireguards?" asked a woman no older than me, but with two terrified little boys clinging to her skirts.

I blurted out before thinking, the fear in her eyes an ember that sparked and burned chaos and fear through the camp faster than the space of a few heartbeats.

Zion must have been listening in, because his mental voice thundered through all of us all at once.

All of them.

CHAPTER
ELEVEN

Where the fuck was Zephyr? Or Shava, for that matter?

"Quick! Spread the word! Start running east!"

There was almost a stampede as children cried and screamed, terrified because their mothers and friends were terrified. Feet pounded all around me, and yet the mass of humanity as a whole moved far too slowly. Scared mothers and children were no match for Fireguards in their prime. It would only be a matter of time before we were surrounded.

A matter of time ended up being less than five minutes.

I could only watch helplessly as the fit men raced past the refugees and pushed them back with whitestone spears, while others came up at their backs when they tried to flee back toward the kingdom. Like cattle, they were herded into a giant circle, Fireguards with gleaming helmets and armor acting as a human wall of flames and steel wherever they turned.

"Keep them there. Don't harm them. We need what's left for our breeding stock, after all."

The queen rode into our camp in a chariot coated with silver and pulled by two white horses with armor that matched the Fireguards, but was pure silver instead of tinged with red and gold. Her demeanor was icy death amongst a sea of flames and terror. She wore an ornate, gaudy white dress with silver armor wrapped around her throat, arms, chest, and legs. A dazzling crown of moonstone and dragonsbane sat on her head, and delicate sandals with jewels were on her feet. Her lips twisted with satisfaction, and I swore I'd never hated anyone in my life as much as I hated her.

Her eyes scanned the crowd. "Where are my sons? Ah, there you are."

The queen acted as this were nothing more than a light dinner party as Zion and Zariah pushed forward toward her. She didn't even react to both of them standing there plain as day, next to each other. The women stared. The Fireguards readjusted their grips on their spears, the shafts wobbling and lowering as they saw two princes for the first time.

The game was over, then.

The queen spoke before either prince could, her cold words dripping from her lips fast and hard like pelting raindrops.

"I forbid you from fighting me. I forbid you from helping M-Mari."

I could tell it pained her to say my real name, and not something more degrading like 'mud rat' or 'bitch,' but instructions had to be specific, didn't they?

Zariah flinched and Zion snarled, golden scales bursting forth as he shifted into his dragon form, unable to control it.

The queen laughed, a light tinkling sound that sounded like glass being scraped across stone. "Oh, and one more thing. I forbid you to move."

Zariah shifted just as the last words left her lips, but the damage was done. My two strong, dragon princes froze on their massive bellies, motionless and paralyzed—two felled monsters prostrated before their conqueror.

Bile rose in my throat and I swallowed it back down.

"That's taken care of." The queen gestured to the small contingent of Fireguards around her who weren't keeping the refugees at spearpoint. Her voice took a hard edge that was nothing like the high-pitched, breathy tone she usually spoke with.

"Lash them down."

A sob tore from my throat as the Fireguards jumped forward, working together and using dozens of ropes to tie Zion and Zariah up, and stake them down into the ground. I winced as the rough ropes cut into the delicate membranes in their wings, forcing them tight against their bodies. How could a mother do this to her children? What defect allowed one to callously watch as a living creature's eyes bugged out in terror and despair?

Zion and Zariah snarled and growled in their throats, but there was nothing they could do as their bindings bit into their skin. Frozen in place, not even a claw twitched.

"That's better. Now that you're settled, you have

permission to move." The queen smiled nastily at her sons. "I want to watch you writhe and squirm as I take back what's mine, and end it by flaying your mud bitch alive."

Zion and Zariah roared with anger, struggling in vain against the ropes. Smoke billowed from under their ropes, which gave off a reddish, copper hue.

Dragonsbane rope. Holy fuck.

The queen turned back to the Fireguards, her hand flicking out in a dismissive gesture.

"Herd them back to whatever remains of the mud and squalor," cried out the queen.

My jaw dropped. It was worse than if she just would have shifted and roasted us all. But this? The queen had taken what I'd said to heart. I'd meant it only to get under skin and make her angry. But she listened. Gods above! If she couldn't breed more dragon sons herself, she'd force her sons to do it.

And it was my fault.

The queen was crazy. Batshit, fucking insane. She—

"No."

The voice was faint in the air, but it was there. And it wasn't from Zion or Zariah. The queen's dainty hand perched above her eyes to peer through the smoke and dust, eyes narrowed.

"Who said that?" she snarled quietly.

The voice was familiar, but even so I prayed it wasn't him.

"I would think after earning a coveted place in my household, you wouldn't be foolish enough to think you are anything other than what you've always been: *mud.*"

I prayed my stupid, sycophant brother Ess would have enough survival instinct and sense of self-preservation that he would stay hidden in the crowd. The queen wouldn't know it was him for sure unless he revealed himself.

So, of course, he did.

My heart soared and clenched as he calmly stepped out of formation toward her, hands gripping his spear nervously but his gaze straight.

"No. These are *our* people. Have you forgotten who makes up your Fireguards? The sons you stole from their mother's arms are the same you educated and trained, which we are happy to do in trade. You educated us. You fed and clothed us."

Heads turned and spear tips drifted downwards. Pride surged in my chest as my father stood in front of the queen, his fist shaking at her face and his jaw set. Pure stubbornness and defiance tensed every muscle in his body.

My stubbornness. My defiance.

Emotion drowned me.

"These people are our mothers and daughters," Ell continued, his voice strong. "Our sisters and few brothers, and unprotected women we hurt whether intentionally or accidentally." He paused, his face twisting with sorrow.

Mother.

Ell turned and looked straight at me. I stopped breathing.

"It's time someone stood up for them." He slammed the butt of his spear into the ground, lifting his chin. "Again, I say, NO."

The queen laughed; one broken, desperate guffaw

that echoed unnaturally loud in the tense silence. "Had that all planned out, did you?" She stepped toward him, grabbing his spear. In one motion she broke it over her knee, scowling. "Did it take you years to come up with such big words? Such big sentiments?"

She pointed at two Fireguards to her left. "Kill him."

The Fireguards jerked, glancing at each other.

"N-no," said the one on the left, shakily.

The queen's eyes narrowed into slits.

"No," said the other on the right.

The queen whipped around but one by one the Fireguards let their spears fall to the ground, a cascading sound of stone hitting charred, blackened earth like the most absurd rainstorm I'd ever heard.

Then came their shouts.

"No."

"No!"

"NO!"

"NO! NO! NO! NO! NO!"

They were chanting now, all in unison, diving into the refugees and picking up the wounded and injured, walking back toward the city. The women joined in and the children raised their fists, shouting with glee in the queen's face as they rode on their shoulders of the same Fireguards who would've beaten them a week ago.

"NO! NO! NO! NO!"

The queen looked fit to burst, her pale face flushing bright red as she gathered her skirts in her fists and ripped the delicate fabric in her fury. An inhuman scream of rage erupted from her throat, and she shifted.

The Fireguards' shouts turned to screams as the enormous silver dragon erupted into being and bellowed, wings unfurling and tail swiping out at anything in reach.

I raced toward Zion and Zariah as did a dozen Fireguards, who quickly and efficiently hacked through the ropes holding the brothers down. With matching roars and ignoring the welts and burn marks ravaging their hides, they shot toward the silver dragon.

A mighty boom like thunder rippled through us as the dragons crashed together. I'd thought Zion and Zariah couldn't fight the queen, but they weren't fighting, were they? My golden dragons kept their bodies between the queen and the Fireguards and refugees, using themselves as literal shields to protect everyone. The queen raged as she tried to duck and dodge around them, but there were two gold dragons to her one silver.

White fire exploded from her mouth, and one of the golden dragons (they were moving too fast for me to keep track!) screamed in agony as he took the full blast to his flank.

I picked up a rock and threw it at the queen, tears coursing down my face. They couldn't fight her, not really! They'd kill themselves at this rate. It wasn't fair!

My princes held firm, and their patient, self-flagellating tactics only threw the queen into more of a fury. In a fit of pique, she took the air and fled back toward the kingdom.

We all watched, confused, as she turned tail and ran, the Fireguards and refugees cheering with victory. My heart wasn't with them; the sinking sensation in my chest refused to let go. What was her plan?

BOOM! BOOM!

The silver dragon shot through the massive hole in the wall the Fireguards had charged through, and fire lit up the sky, flaring high up to the dome. It served no protection at all now that the dragon was *inside the city*.

YOU HAVE TO STOP HER! PROTECT YOUR PEOPLE! I screamed mentally, but they were both in the air already, wings pumping hard as they took off after the queen. I turned toward Ell, who was racing toward me.

We seized each other in a tight embrace, tears pricking at the corner of my eyes. There would be plenty of time for sobbing reunions later. For now, I had to keep it together and keep these people safe.

I said, "Get everyone close to the cliffs, and out of the open air. At least it's some cover."

Ell nodded and barked out orders to the other Fireguards, and quickly we had everyone moving toward the large outcropping of rocks, which provided cover and a view of the devastation going back on in the kingdom.

Zion and Zariah were nipping at the queen's heels, unable to attack but certainly able to annoy and frustrate her. They knocked down as much of the outer wall as they could, trying to herd the queen out of the kingdom's bounds and away from the city. Single-minded in her mad quest to destroy, she refused. It was almost as if she were trying to kill everyone inside.

"Come on, I'll take you. The others will look after them all." Ell gently took my elbow and gestured to the queen's chariot, which sat innocently a few feet away, the two white horses calm and docile.

I nodded, too thankful to muster up any words. Ell

helped me step up into the chariot, pressing himself in behind me. He squared his hips and shoulders so I was locked protectively in front of him, and I grasped the edge of the silver chariot with my fingertips. Ell grabbed the reins and snapped them, the horses jerking to attention. My heart pounded as we flew across the charred land back toward the kingdom, rocking and bumping wildly. I was glad for Ell's strong, steady presence holding me in place, or I'd have surely been thrown from the chariot and trampled on the rocks.

My throat tightened for a reason other than fear or anxiety. Was this what Azalea and Leilani had had—a father always by their side to defend and guide? Warmth spread through my body that had nothing to do with Ell's chest pressed protectively against my back.

Focus, Mari.

Boys! Divide and conquer! I forced the thought to them with every bit of will I had. The golden dragons twitched in midair, then flipped their strategy. One of my boys nipped continuously at the queen's wings, forcing her to fly around and around in circles as he subtly moved her out away from the city center. The other dragon stood guard between the two 'playing' dragons (because nipping at your wings apparently didn't count as fighting), ensuring the people in the quarters could run to safety.

And run, they did.

Ell guided the chariot toward the biggest hole in the west side of the wall, hordes of terrified people from all quarters and walks of life streaming past us. There were bakers from the bread district, artists from the artisan quarter, and masons from the stone quarter. Men, women, and children pushed past, crying and yelling, fear widening the whites in their eyes.

A niggling thought pulled at the back of my mind. *Where the fuck was Zephyr?*

All thoughts in my head came to a screeching halt as the silver dragon screamed in distress. The sound was devastating and threw every living creature to their bellies. The horses pulling our chariot screamed in fear and broke from their harness, sending us careening toward the ground. Ell pinned me to his chest and tucked and rolled, using his body to shield me as we smashed against the hard, black earth. His weight pinned me down hard, and I struggled to free myself. Twin flashes of gold winked before my gaze, but I could've been hallucinating. My eyes were fuzzy and it was hard to see. Ell's arms fell away limply from me.

The queen's silver dragon screamed in frustration again, and I thought my head would explode. Nothing existed beyond the pain and agony. Was it from the fall, or the dragon? Was I dying?

Magick pounded around me in an angry torrent, setting my hair on edge and crawling over my skin. I held my breath as nausea clawed at my gut. After a few seconds, it passed like a strong gust of wind that had run its course.

"Ell, can you shift a bit? I need to get up."

Ell didn't move from on top of me. I flipped over on my back, unprepared to come face-to-face with a head that looked like it had been thrown through a meat grinder and bent at an unnatural angle at the neck.

I twisted my own head to the side and just

managed not to vomit all over myself. With shaking hands, I dragged myself from underneath my father, the pads of my fingertips bleeding at raw from the jagged stones underneath me.

"Ell. ELL!"

I knew he was dead. An idiot knew he was dead. But I couldn't let go. I couldn't tear from gaze from his raw face, blood oozing down to collect in a dark pool.

But I had to. I *had* to. There was nothing else to be done for him. I would come back and collect him. I'd build him a proper grave. I'd bring my mother to it.

Mother.

I stumbled toward the city on legs that didn't work right. Glancing up, I faltered.

The walls were gone, destroyed by the power of the dragon's distress call. Rubble lay everywhere, and as I watched, the mighty dome cracked in half. One of the golden dragons gave a roar of warning, but it was too late.

I watched with horror as the dome collapsed.

The plume of dust and debris shot a mile high into the air, obscuring the entire kingdom, including all three dragons. My entire life exploded before my eyes and disappeared behind a gray curtain so thick it was like the entire kingdom had disappeared. This was a nightmare. I had to be dreaming. Surely, this wasn't real.

Mari—

"NO!"

I don't know which of my princes had called out to me, but fear shot through my veins as his voice cut off abruptly in my head.

ZION! ZARIAH!

No answer.

I screamed until it hurt and ran as fast as I could, refusing to lose anyone else. Leilani. My mother. Zion. Azalea. Zariah. Even Freesia. Heather and Hyacinthe. Even my goddamn brother.

NO NO NO NO NO NO NO NO NO.

I chanted the word in my head as fiercely as the Fireguards and refugees had, ignoring the burn in my lungs and the sting in my eyes. Every able member in the kingdom ran past me, a man I didn't know grabbed me by my shoulders and dragged me with him.

"There's nothing for it back there! They're all gone! You have to come this way!"

I raged and screamed and tried to kick the well-meaning, portly man in his shins, but another man much taller and stronger grabbed my legs and together they hauled me in the opposite direction.

I kept trying to scream but the roar was too loud—of the city collapsing in on itself, and the horrific plume of debris that raced across the landscape: right toward us.

Screams of terror filled my ears as we ran, my body going numb as it bounced against the back of the man lessening his own chances of survival to ensure mine.

Another theme in my life.

I wanted to die then. With a huge surge of adrenaline, I wrenched myself away from the man and fell off his shoulder and onto the ground. Pain exploded up my knees as it took the brunt of my fall. He turned back and tried to grab me, and I kicked at him.

"On your own head be it!" the tall man scoffed, running away as the dust cloud was only feet away. The portly man stayed, crouching next to me and ripping the white apron that covered his ample belly in half. The first part he tied around his face, the second one he offered to me.

I gawked at him.

"Put it on! We can't avoid it now!"

I pushed the cloth over my nose and mouth right as the debris cloud hit us.

Chapter
Twelve

The man's hand on my back pushed me down gently into a fetal position. Together we waited out the worst of it, my breaths hot and heavy against the rough, homespun fabric that was nonetheless nicer than anything I'd ever had to wear in the mud district.

It smelled like bread and sugar, and I breathed it in, trying to pretend I was anywhere else.

After what felt like a lifetime, I raised my head. The sun had just been trying to rise as Ell had helped me into the chariot, and it was still blocked, even if the dome was gone. Everything had an odd, gold glow. The air was thick and hard to breathe. I was covered in gray ash, and so was the man next to me. Everything was covered. The air was littered with more, falling down on us continuously like rain.

We're all demons now, I thought, on the brink of hysteria.

I stumbled to my feet, leaving the man to find his

own way out. He called after me, but I kept moving in the direction I prayed led toward the city. I couldn't see more than a few feet in front of me.

ZION! ZARIAH!

As the dust continued to settle around me, a large, scaled lump crawled toward me, staggering to the side and falling before righting its massive body.

Was it Zion? Zariah? I didn't care which; I just wanted them both to be safe!

"Zion! Zariah!"

I raced toward the dragon covered in a thick layer of ash like I was, wanting nothing more than to feel his scales heat my cold, blistered fingers.

The dragon had its head buried into the ground rubbing its snout and face furiously against the ground in an effort to clear ash and soot from its eyes.

"Let me—"

I reached and the dragon lunged, fangs bared. Grim realization shot through me as I realized the truth too late: this wasn't my dragon. It was the queen.

A hand seized my collar and yanked me backwards, just out of reach of the queen's fangs. I spun around to see the portly baker, covered in ash but his eyes wide in fear at seeing a dragon up close and personal.

"H-here, dragon tamer," he whispered, withdrawing a small knife from his pocket. I took with plunging hope. It was a toothpick of annoyance compared to a dragon's tough scales.

"Thanks," I said anyway. "Now get away."

I didn't want him to see me get torn limb from limb, after all. The man scurried away, disappearing quickly in the debris cloud. He could have stopped ten feet away and I wouldn't have known with how thick and polluted the air was.

The dragon huffed as I wielded the pathetic knife against her, smoke curling out from her mouth. She swiped her claws at me and easily knocked the blade from my hands, sending it skittering away and lost in the void of dust.

Well done, Mari.

The queen pounced and I tripped, falling on my back and raising my arms protectively over my face. Instinctively, I lashed out with the only thing I had left: my fingernails. I scoured her nose and eyes as best I could, taking brief satisfaction in her squeal of pain as she reared back, not expecting me to fight back with my own hands.

The dragon stomped and huffed backward, frantically rubbing her eyes furiously. Blood streaked down her cheeks, and I smiled.

Take that, bitch.

She stalked forward again, and I raised my hands threateningly. She stumbled as if wounded or drunk. I watched in confusion as her massive body slammed to the ground, her crown from earlier detaching from where it had been lodged between her ears and rolling across the ground and coming to rest at my feet.

Slowly, torturously, she shifted back into her human form. Inch by inch, smooth human flesh replaced hard, silver scales. Her fangs retracted back into her gums, and her black, deadly claws became harmless human nails once more.

Well, not harmless. Look what I'd done with mine.

My mind whirled, confused at how I'd beaten her with so little effort. The memory of our deal in the palace came back to me, her snug voice echoing in my mind.

"*Is the fight to the death, then?*" *I had asked, standing in front of her throne in my battle clothes.*

The queen tittered, trying to sound like a bird. To me, she sounded like a cawing crow. "*How barbaric. First blood will suffice.*"

First blood. First *blood*.

Laughter bubbled from my lips, because it was so utterly simple. All this time, all either of us had to do was draw blood from the other? Grimly, I mentally thanked the queen for slamming me into the wall the other day, and not ripping me open with her claws. Hell, all she'd needed to do was scratch my pinky.

It didn't matter now.

"*And if I win?*"

A slow, sick smile spread across her face, as though such a thing were laughable. "*I suppose I'd have to relinquish my crown if such a thing were to happen.*"

I stared at the crown at my feet. It was mostly covered in ash now, like everything else, but parts of it still glittered despite the heavy smog in the air. I let it lay and raced past her, unable to spare her any more concern when Zariah and Zion were silent in my head.

The repercussions of this would be dealt with later.

Zion! Zariah!

I couldn't see more than five feet or so in front of me, and everything was covered in an ashy haze. The ash clung to my hair, my clothes, and my lungs with every breath I took. As I neared the destroyed wall, I was forced to slow down and carefully pick my way through the mess and debris.

It had been eerily quiet since the wall fell, but that

was changing. The moans and cries of hundreds of wounded filled the air one by one, desperate for help. I steadfastly kept going, knowing that I'd be able to help everyone else more if I could make sure Zion and Zariah were all right. In their dragon forms, they'd easily be able to lift the rubble and save everyone!

Zion! Zariah!

I stumbled into my first dragon before I saw him, tripping over a large golden tail and falling hard on my hip. Wincing, I brushed the ash away to reveal golden scales underneath.

"Are you all right? Are you hurt?"

I didn't know which prince it was, but it didn't matter. I followed the ash-covered lumps until I found his head, and stroked the ridge above his eyes gently. Massive slabs of broken dragonstone covered his body, likely from the dome's collapse. His position was odd and twisted, like he'd been hunched over something right as everything had gone to hell, and now he was stuck. It looked horribly uncomfortable.

"Wake up. Please." My voice wavered, and I took a deep breath to collect myself. I had to be strong.

Golden eyes cracked open at me, slit like a cat's.

"Hey. Are you in there?"

Mari.

Zion's tired, pained gaze met mine. The dragon groaned, and tried to get his feet under him, pushing down against the ground to try and gain purchase. Golden scales covered in ash rippled and strained, but the slabs on top of him only moved a few inches. The dragon sagged back down, defeated.

"Don't worry. We'll get you out. Are you OK otherwise?" I asked, desperately praying he was.

His large eyes blinked at me.

Tired, he managed.

I kept stroking down the ridge of his snout. "I know. Just hang in there. I'm going to find Zariah, and he'll get you out of here. He's more used to his dragon form than you are, so I'm sure he's fine. Everything will be all right."

Don't cry. Don't cry.

Leaving Zion buried there was one of the hardest things I'd ever done, but I couldn't save him by myself. I couldn't even begin to try.

Zariah! ZARIAH!

I spun around, but there was no telling where a dragon was buried underneath all of this mess and confusion. If only I could *see*, then this wouldn't be so hard!

ZARIAH! I called again, desperation digging a hole in my heart.

Stop screaming. I hear you.

Relief flooded my veins and I staggered, my knees weak at hearing him alive and well enough to sass me with that cocky tone.

Where are you? Zion needs help! He's trapped under the rubble!

Zariah swore in my mind. **All right. Stay where you are; I can scent you out.**

I hurried back to Zion's side, squeezing back tears as other survivors straggled around me. Sitting down on the dusty ground next to Zion, I put my hand flat on his face and tried to find a clean path of my clothes to wipe the grime from his eyes and snout. My clothes were covered in dust, my fingers curling into fists as I realized not a single inch of me was clean.

No one was clean. The only clean streaks of skin around me were the tears tacks on everyone's faces, cutting clean paths down their cheeks from sorrow and fear.

His eyes cracked open again, and his tongue shot out, finding a gash on the underside of my arm I hadn't noticed and licking the blood off.

I winced at the pain, but didn't pull away. The cut healed, and the fog in his eyes lifted a bit.

Mari. I'm sorry. You should help others.

His gaze was fixed on the dozens of people walking toward the rubble, all of us appearing like ghosts covered in gray ash. If the circumstances were any different, it would have made my heart soar to watch how they all worked together to free the others who were still trapped. Artisan quarter, bread quarter, stone quarter, mud quarter ... you couldn't tell under the dirt and grime. We were all the same.

But I couldn't bring myself to leave Zion's side.

The people around me muttered and skipped nervously away as Zariah's massive form crawled out of the haze, his eyes taking in Zion's situation with a scoff.

We had plenty of warning it was going to fall. You are slow.

My mouth parted to deliver a biting retort. Now wasn't the time for insults! But Zion huffed, a sound that could have been mistaken for a laugh. Otherwise, he didn't defend himself.

Zariah carefully grasped the top chunks in his claws and shifted them slightly, pushing them to the side to take the weight off Zion without accidentally crushing anyone nearby. In quick succession he had five pieces off, only to reveal a massive section of the dome bigger than him. That was what truly had Zion pinned.

"Oh no." I didn't see how Zariah could lift it. Not in this lifetime. Not in a thousand lifetimes. Tears streamed down my cheeks, leaving clean tracks where the ash ran down my face.

"Over here! We need to free the dragon! Then it can help us!"

I craned around to look over my shoulder. The portly man from before gestured toward me, his face blackened by ash and grime.

We were all mud boys and girls, now.

"My children! They're gone! Where are my babies?" screamed another woman, her hands raw and bloody from digging through the rubble.

"Free the dragon and then both of them can help us!" the baker argued. People around him nodded, and swarmed Zion and Zariah. They all lined up to grip a piece of the massive dome, and more came running. Soon, nearly fifty people were lined up to try and help.

Tell them to leave a space in the middle for me, and you give the countdown, Zariah ordered.

I passed the message along and the crowd parted, allowing Zariah into the middle to grasp the main part of the slab in his claws. The massive dragon looked odd standing on his hind legs, his wings folded against his back like a cape. It was surreal to see him standing side by side with people from the kingdom from all walks of life.

"Ok," I began, trying to sound strong. "On three. One ... two ... three!"

Everyone pushed and grunted. The muscles in

Zariah's back strained and flexed, and slowly, ever so slowly, the massive stone lifted.

Keep going! If we get it high enough he can roll out!

Zion's gaze fluttered up to me. **I can't roll out,** he argued.

Zariah growled, and the stone faltered. **Goddamnit, now! We can't hold it for long!**

I didn't understand what the issue was; all Zariah had to do was roll. Even if he was injured, surely he could summon the strength for this!

I can't, he stubbornly insisted.

Zariah bellowed and dropped the slab, the human help scattering as it fell back on Zion with a heavy thump. Zion roared in pain as it slammed into his back, and I'd never felt more helpless than I had in that moment.

Was what his problem? Can't—

"THERE IS ANOTHER DRAGON! HIDE!"

My heart dropped into my chest. The last thing we needed was for the queen to recover and shift, destroying whatever meager crumbs were left of this kingdom. Zariah growled and leaped over his fallen brother and most of the crowd, landing with a large thump that shook the ground. His dragon ears were slicked back against his skull as he growled, waiting.

But it wasn't the queen who stepped out of the haze.

It was a *fourth* dragon.

CHAPTER
THIRTEEN

Massive and black, it was easily twice as big as Zion and Zariah. From the tip of his ears scales to his wings and claws, the dragon seemed a shadow of death. All was dark except for his eyes, which glowed silver. And his fangs, which were pristine and white.

He roared in challenge. **Give me my mate!**

Ok. That wasn't exactly what I thought it would say. Though to be honest, I hadn't expected it to speak at all! Zariah's head tilted to the side, mirroring the confusion we all felt.

She is here! I smell her! The black dragon threw his head in the air, looking wildly left and right. **I heard her distress call across the desert! What have you done to her?!**

Distress call? Across the desert?

The black dragon pounced and Zariah snarled, leaping to put himself in front of me. But the newcomer hadn't put one claw in my direction—he'd leaped to the side, and let out a roar of despair, nudging an ash-covered lump on the ground.

The queen.

The dragon shifted into a man, albeit one that wasn't ... as man like as Zion and Zariah. He humanoid in shape, but covered in black scales from the waist down ... his naked waist. I blushed and kept my eyes up, and boy, was there plenty to see up.

From the waist up, his skin looked more like human skin, but with an odd shimmer that revealed iridescent scales just underneath the surface. White fangs hung from his top lip, and he had black wings in this form! His hair was black and straight, falling to the small of his back.

"What did you do to my mate?" he growled, picking up the former queen in his arms and carrying her like she weighed no more than a flower.

Zariah growled back. **My *mother* went and attacked the kingdom and its people. We are in crisis. Your strength would be welcome to help any survivors.**

The dragon man frowned, looking down at the limp, ashen figure of the queen in his arms. "My mate is more important than your problems. And if she did all of this, it was not her fault."

The indignant guffaw left my mouth before I could help it.

The dragon man glared at me, tightening his grip on the queen. "Dragons who do not find their mate go mad." He shot a look at Zariah and me. "You are fortunate to have found yours. I will take mine now. Goodbye."

He turned to leave and I raced forward. "Wait!

No! Please, my other mate is trapped below the rubble. Zariah in his dragon form isn't strong enough to lift it. And ... and your ... mate is not strong enough to survive the journey. Stay here awhile and let her rest."

The dragon man's heavy brow furrowed, studying Zariah and I. "You are draklings. Where is your elder?"

I didn't understand either or those words, and a quick glance at Zariah revealed he didn't either. "She had command over her sons," I tried out, pointing to her in his arms. "Is that what you mean?"

The dragon man bent down and sniffed his mate "First generation. A curse then? You know nothing, I wager."

Reluctantly, and gently, he laid her down and propped her up against a chunk of marble that had to have come from the palace or the bathing chambers. How had it gotten all the way here? We were a far cry away from the pristine, clean hallways of the castle.

"I will help you because you are stupid and weak, and my mate needs rest."

Zariah chuffed at this, the scales on his ears flaring up as he growled at the insult. I pressed my palm against his side, imploring him to stay silent. We needed this dragon's help. He had knowledge of the curse and about dragons!

Giving the gawking people a dark look, he backed up and shifted back into his massive dragon form. He approached the huge slab of the dome that kept Zion trapped, growling as he sniffed the stuck prince over. With a jerk of his head to Zariah, both dragons took their places while I gestured for everyone else to back up.

On three then, the black dragon commanded. **One. Two. THREE!**

Both dragons heaved and groaned, their combined strength enough to push the slab up away, flipping it over so it landed ten feet away. Both dragons huffed and puffed in great steamy heaves of breath, but I rushed forward toward Zion, who was still in his odd, crouched position. I put a hand to my mouth at the crumpled, twisted remains of his wings.

Ruined.

Someone was crying. Was it me? No, that wasn't accurate. Many people were crying. No, not people ... children.

Zion carefully and laboriously got his legs under him, and finally lifted his front and back legs. The black dragon rushed to support him, sticking his snout and then his entire body underneath Zion's to support his weight. When I saw what Zion had been protecting so ardently, I started crying.

Kids.

So many kids.

People around me cried out and rushed forward as at least three dozen children swarmed out from underneath Zion's massive frame, finding their parents and loved ones. Zariah helped the black dragon support Zion's weight as they settled him back down again, a whine leaving Zariah's throat as he sniffed the ruin of Zion's wings.

The black dragon turned his head toward the three of us. **You are mates, the three of you. You can heal him, but I don't know if it will be enough to allow him to fly again.**

I nodded, not trusting myself to speak. If my mouth opened, I'd start openly sobbing.

I wish to rest with my mate now.

Zariah's ears flicked up. **Take any room you want in the castle up there.** He pointed one claw above us, up toward the Seat.

Delicately, the black dragon leaned over and took the queen in his claws, his wings beating the ground on either side of him. Men and women clutched their children to them and covered their heads as dust buffeted all of us. With a running leap, he jumped into the sky and took off, quickly disappearing above, somewhere in the Seat. I imagined the Nobles were all having heart attacks as the great black dragon swooped toward them, but I couldn't be bothered to care.

My head shook side to side, as if my body still couldn't process everything that had happened. The queen—how do I not call her the queen—would be gone soon, and there was another large dragon here. My boys didn't seem to mind. And had the black dragon indirectly told me to feed Zion my blood? Or Zariah's?

We hadn't even gotten the other dragon's *name*.

"Shift back, and we can move you," I cajoled him. Just like when the queen had been injured, it took a while for Zion's large dragon form to fold inwards and let his human one come through. He was covered in so much dust and grime it was difficult to tell if he was still injured in this form.

Get him on my back and hold him, Zariah told me, putting his head and neck down on the ground so we could climb up. A few people rushed forward to help me support Zion's weight, mostly parents of the children. In short order I was clutching to Zariah's neck spikes, Zion's limp body held in place in front of me.

"Do you have a place in mind?" I yelled out to Zariah, but he simply took off into the air. We cleared the dust and haze that hung over the kingdom, my lungs clearing as I finally took a gulp of fresh, clean air. From above, it was heart-wrenching to see just how much damage the kingdom had suffered with the collapse of the dome. There was a glimmer of hope, however. The castle hadn't been completely covered by the dome, so when it fell, it didn't take much damage.

Which meant the Seat itself had only taken limited damage.

I tried to quell the frustration in my heart, but it was no use. It wasn't fair the poorest once against got the shaft, while those rich and fed were spared most of the horrors.

I can smell your anger, Zariah scolded me. **Besides, I plan to put as many people in the Seat and castle as I can until we can clean up and clear the quarters. All of them, if I can.**

Warmth spread through my body, and my eyes closed in thanks. Both of my princes were protective and kind in their own ways. Zariah would bully the Nobles into accepting the refugees and the others displaced, and Zion would sacrifice himself to save children.

I loved them both desperately.

As Zariah descended toward the castle's front lawn, it was obvious the Nobles weren't sitting on their bottoms. They moved about with efficiency, gathering blankets and food and clothes, and tying them up in bundles. And in the middle of this project stood Freesia, the hem of her gown torn and a large smudge of blood and dirt on her left cheek.

Everyone scattered as Zariah's massive form went in to land, but Freesia rushed forward. "Oh, finally! This will be helpful. We were stuck trying to figure out how to fix the elevators, but this solves that." She huffed. "The other dragon ignored me when I asked him to help."

Once again, I was struck by how fearless Freesia truly was, to just casually walk up to a strange dragon and demand help. A smile twitched my lips.

"Let me get Zion settled, then we will help you," I told her, looking around at her organization. "This is ... impressive!"

Freesia smirked. "Well, some upstart mud girl told me I was intelligent. So ... I was." She blushed, and glanced away, folding her arms across her chest.

Zariah shifted and caught his brother, no one batting an eye at their nakedness. Desperate times made you reevaluate your priorities.

"Yes, well, hurry back. We can ferry people up here for safety, but there's likely still many trapped that need to be freed." She snapped her fingers. "That reminds me: your brother has taken charge of your mother. They're somewhere inside the castle."

At my indignant look, she rolled her eyes. "It was that or leave her alone, since Ell went with you."

A bolt of guilt shot through me at the reminder. Ell was still below the Seat, his body likely right where I'd left him. Would the tally never end?

"Oh! And we're pretty sure you broke the curse," she continued. "At one point up here, all of the infected

Nobles fell unconscious, and ash just ... fell off their bodies. When they woke up, they looked normal!"

I stared at her in shock, then fell toward Freesia and seized her in a massive hug, my eyes heating with emotion. "Thank you," I breathed out, unable to truly express how I'd felt.

She stiffened at my touch, her arms awkwardly wrapping around me after a moment. "Yes, well ... I'm not the one who broke the curse."

Zariah cleared his throat, and I broke away. "I will come back to help you. We have to take care of Zion first. See you soon."

Freesia nodded, and I followed Zariah up the chipped stone steps and into the palace. The castle had sustained damage, but it was still a usable structure that could hold a lot of people. Zariah carried his brother in his arms, a look of grim determination on his face. The trip to their tower seemed to take only seconds, though I knew that was impossible. I had a lot on my mind. Had I broken the curse? And how? It was wonderful news the Nobles were cured, and that we didn't have to worry about anyone else shifting into a demon! But what about Zariah and Zion? And the queen? All of them still had their dragon powers.

Zariah laid Zion down gently on the bed and took a knee in front of it. I climbed onto the mattress next to Zion, smoothing his hair back out of his eyes.

"The black dragon said our blood would heal him," I reminded Zariah.

Zariah shot me a glare. "No way. I'm doing this."

Before I could protest, he grabbed a small knife from the bedside table and dragged it over his forearm.

Blood welled from the wound, and he pushed it toward Zion's mouth.

"I don't think—" I began, only to cut myself off as Zion jerked, then lunged at the bleeding arm in front of him. Fangs descended from his mouth and bit down hard into his brother's arm. Zariah winced, but didn't jerk away.

"Is he ... feeding?" I asked warily.

Zariah blinked slowly. "Yeah. I feel ... Phew. That's a lot."

Zariah slumped over the bed, yawning as Zion drank and drank. The paler Zariah got, the more worried I became, even as color began to flush Zion's face again.

"That's enough," I chastised Zion.

He growled at me, the sound distorted coming from his human throat.

I doubled down. **Enough!** I shouted through our bond, and pushed his face away. Zion detached from Zariah with a pop, and rolled toward me, wrapping his arms around my body and snuggling into my chest.

"I guess he's good," I said lamely, now trapped in bed.

Zariah laughed and yawned as he sat up, wiping his forearm and pulling a pair of pants on from underneath his bed. "You stay here with him. I'll help with the recovery efforts."

"What?!" I protested. "No! I want to help! You can't—"

Zariah put a hand on Zion's side, and the other on my head. "Mari, please. I can't focus on helping my people unless I know Zion is taken care of. That you are taken care of. Make sure he eats and recovers. Make sure *you* eat and recover. Please, for me?"

Urgh, I couldn't resist when he gave me those puppy dog eyes.

"Fine," I relented. It wasn't like I could go anywhere anyway. Zion had me in an iron grip.

"Good." Zariah grinned. "I'll be back when the job's done."

My jaw dropped as he climbed up the window and jumped out. A flash of gold scales later and the dragon was in the air.

"Show off," I muttered darkly, turning in Zion's arms so we were face to face. "Are you feeling better?"

He squeezed me tighter, his lips and teeth dragging against my neck. Zion's pelvis pushed against mine, letting me know exactly where his thoughts lay, conscious or not. Fangs descended from his gums and pricked at my sensitive flesh.

"I probably can't fly," he said, so nonchalantly I almost missed it.

"What?! Your wings?" I gasped, wanting to know more but Zion was clearly focused on other things.

"It was worth it. It's all worth it if I never fly again," he slurred, almost as if he were drunk.

"I think you need to calm down," I grit out, feeling him poke into my backside.

Zion bit down on my neck, hard.

I couldn't scream—every muscle in my body tensed instead as his fangs pierced my neck and he drank from me. I didn't want to deny him what he so desperately needed since he couldn't suck Zariah dry; Zariah was needed to help in the recovery efforts.

And yet through the pain, something else was

blooming. The wound burned, sending warmth and fire straight to my core and igniting my blood. The initial pain had only lasted a moment, a brief flash that was now numbing over and leaving behind a delicious, wonderful floating sensation, similar to when he'd made my limbs go numb in the past. Without thinking about it, I pushed my hips against his.

"Down," he rumbled, detaching from my neck and pushing me onto the bed on my stomach.

I barely had a moment to breathe before my pants were around my ankles and he was rubbing up behind me. The wound on my neck bled and ached and burned, but it felt raw and cathartic.

Zion leaned over me, his tongue rougher than normal as it dragged over the wound. The pain faded into that blissful numbness as the wound healed.

"My marks. My mate," he growled into my ear.

Sounded good to me.

His arm wrapped around my neck and pushed me up, arching my back up against him as he lined himself up with my center, and thrust in.

We both moaned at the contact, the pain and pressure a dangerous aphrodisiac as he set a brutal pace. Dark blood smeared across his forearm, right under my chin. My tongue reached out and licked it, wondering what the big fuss was about the blood.

"You naughty flower," he chastised me, tightening his grip on my neck. Spicy heat blossomed across my tongue, and he yanked my head back to give me a rough, passionate kiss upside down. Never once did his hips cease snapping against me, driving him further and further into me.

Gold scales erupted across his body, winking and

flashing as the sun streaming through the windows hit them at different angles. The bedsheet became hopelessly tangled and hot, so we flung off the bed. His weight on top of me increased as his skin heated to an inferno against mine.

A small warning bell went off in my head, but I didn't want to stop. The growing pressure and weight was soothing, like a heavy blanket. His cock inside of me swelled as he thrust in and out, both of us slick with heat and mad with desire. I—

IF YOU FUCK HER IN YOUR DRAGON FORM, I WILL RIP OFF WHATEVER SCRAPS OF YOUR WINGS ARE LEFT.

Zariah's angry tirade snapped me back to reality, allowing my brain to catch up with what we were doing. Zion, however, roared in defiance, his body halfway between man and dragon. I twisted around and elbowed him as hard as I could.

He made a funny 'oomph' sound and rolled off the bed, his scales and fangs vanishing in an instant.

I scrambled to look over the edge, afraid he'd hurt himself further. We shouldn't have even been doing what we'd been doing—I'd promised Zariah I'd make him rest, not taunt his dragon with some hanky-panky!

"Zion! Are you all right?"

From his spot on the floor he propped himself up on his elbows, dark hair eschew and still a bit of his dragon's feral gold in his eyes.

"I ... fuck" was all he managed, his breaths coming in gasps. His chest heaved up and down as he fought for control. "Yeah. Fine. Shit, that was a bad idea. Mari, I'm so sorry, I—"

I put a hand up, not wanting to hear it. "It's fine. I'm glad there's two of you because it helps you check each other. That would probably have been bad," I finished lamely.

His eyes flashed gold one more time before fading into their normal black. Zion flushed and looked away, running an embarrassed hand through his hair.

"Yeah, probably."

"Probably," I added after him, though I was mostly trying to convince myself.

An awkward silence surrounded us, compelling me to fill it with something.

"Maybe ..." I began, hesitating. I couldn't believe I was about to say it, but I plunged on anyway. "Maybe ... someday. When you're both here to watch each other?"

Zion's eyes flashed gold again, a telltale sign of lust. He crawled up the side of the bed toward me on his hands and knees.

"Careful, flower. Don't want to burn your petals."

The adrenaline of what had almost been drained through my system, leaving me empty. His arms wrapped around me and he tucked me into his chest. He smelled like ashes and spice, like rain and rebirth. The steady rhythm of his heartbeat quickly lulled me into a deep sleep.

CHAPTER FOURTEEN

When I woke, it was Zion nuzzling my neck with his nose and holding a small cake to my lips.

I bit down without thinking, my stomach rumbled with hunger. Sugar and flavor exploded in my mouth, waking me more effectively. I sat up in bed, a little sore but feeling more recovered than I thought possible.

"Here, there's more." Zion slipped out of bed and picked up a plate, setting it on my knees. An entire selection of little cakes and fruits met my eyes, the smells divine.

"Enough about me! How are you?" I demanded instead, looking around and frowning. "And where's Zariah?"

Zion popped a cake in his own mouth, brows furrowed. "If I know him, he will need to be relieved. Otherwise, he'll work himself to exhaustion."

I moved the plate and got out of bed, running my

hands through my hair to comb it and quickly threw it in a braid. "And how do you feel?"

Zion winced. "My back is still on fire. I'm afraid to shift and see what the damage is."

That was understandable.

"Let's go. I need to see my mother, and let's find Zariah." I paused. "You haven't seen Shava or Zephyr, have you? They disappeared right before the queen attacked."

Zion huffed. "No, I haven't."

Well then, just another thing to add to the list.

Zion and I emerged from our tower, both of us in awe at the hustle and bustle of the castle. Even before the attack, the halls hadn't been full of people like this! Servants and bakers hustled back and forth indiscriminately, feeding the hordes of people lodged in every available room. Stone masons were gathered in clusters, pointing at damaged sections of the castle and arguing over the best way to proceed. Two children clipped my ankle as they ran past me, intent on their game of tag.

Zion stopped, taking it all in. "I've never ... seen it this lively," he remarked, in awe. "It's ... beautiful."

I remembered how either he or his brother had said that they weren't allowed to play with other children growing up. Had the entire castle been isolated to keep their secret? How lonely! I grabbed his hand, giving it a squeeze. It was incredible to see how people came together in the wake of tragedy and brought out the best in each other. At the same time, I couldn't help but hate that it took such heartbreak to make it happen. No one gave a shit when everything was fine, but present them a situation so heinous to their sensibilities that they are forced to take the other side, and see what happened.

Imagine what the world would be like if we had that mentality every day.

"Mari? MARI!"

A familiar voice caught my attention and I turned, running straight into Leilani. She looked a little worse for wear with soot in her blonde hair, but we all looked awful at the moment.

"You did it! I'm so sorry I didn't believe you. You forgive me, right?" Her desperate plea went straight to my heart, and I hugged her. I'd never considered myself a touchy-feely person, but I couldn't help it. I wanted to grab everyone close to me and never let go.

"Of course!" I shouted back, my voice muffled by her hair.

Leilani drew back, sniffing. "Your mother is here! Ess was doing his best, but it's obvious he's never done anything for himself in his life, so naturally he can't take care of anyone else. I'll take you!"

I shot Zion an apologetic look, but he waved me away with a small smile and immediately was surrounded by a group of squawking Nobles. Better him than me, I supposed.

"Come on! She's just down this hallway!"

I never had really managed to memorize the layout of the castle, but I needn't have worried; Leilani clearly knew exactly where she was going.

"The second door on the right. She—oh." Leilani drew up short at seeing a grim figure standing guard out front. My eyes narrowed as I set eyes on my estranged brother.

"Ess," I grit out. "I came to see our mother."

He stuck his nose in the air, arms crossed over his chest. "She's sleeping. And she hasn't slept in a while. I can't let you go in there."

Irritation and anger flared in my veins. "You can't keep me from her," I bit out, trying to keep my voice down if what he said was true. How dare he try to ban me from seeing her! Who the hell did he think he was?

Emotion flared in his eyes, even as his hands balls into fists at his sides and he stood between me and the door. I'd murder him. I'd put him in the ground so fast—

Leilani stepped in, putting a calming hand on my arm. "No one is trying to stop anyone here. Ess, you're just trying to look out for her, right? She is mother to both of you, after all."

My throat bobbed, my stubbornness not wanting to give up the fight, but my mind arguing that I would do the same in our positions were reversed. The fire in Ess's eyes wasn't staged, after all. Maybe he was doing the best he could, and he truly believed my presence would disturb her from her rest. If the positions were reversed, I'd act exactly like him. If we were both on the side of protecting our mother, then that was a good thing. Even if I wasn't quite ready to give up the title of sole protector myself yet, I could see the logic of having someone around to help.

"Fine," I managed, staring at the ground and crossing my arms.

Leilani blinked, taking in both of us in similar positions. "Oh wow. Yeah, I see it now." She giggled, then cleared her throat. An awkward silence stretched between the three of us.

"You're so busy being the dragon girl. Maybe spend some time with her," Ess muttered.

My jaw dropped at the audacity. He wanted to point fingers? Fine by me. "And where were you the last twenty-one years while I had to fight and scrape for every morsel of food that went into her mouth? I ought to knock some of your teeth out," I whispered furiously, taking a step forward.

His eyes widened, his back against the door. "You wouldn't dare. The queen—"

"Was claimed by a massive black dragon and isn't queen anymore," I corrected him. I shouldn't have enjoyed the shocked look on his face so much, but no one was perfect.

"B-b-but I—" he stuttered.

"Mari, let's come back later after your mother has rested." Leilani took my elbow and steered me away from my idiot brother. I was sad he turned out to be such a softy, but I couldn't blame him. He'd never worried about his next meal, after all. I should be thankful his life had been so easy compared to mine. It was interesting to contrast him to Zephyr, who only seemed hardened by his time in the Seat.

"I don't want to leave. But you may stay with me here." I pulled Leilani over to a small couch on the other side of the room. My brother tightened his stance in front of the door, and I sighed, holding my hands out helplessly.

"Look, I promise not to wake her up. Can't we just let the past be the past, and go from here? Having someone else help me with her is welcome." The words tasted a bit ashy in my mouth, but I forced them out.

Ess's posture relaxed. Slightly.

"Well, if you're staying for a bit, I'm taking a break," he conceded.

Ess turned on his heel and walked away, finally leaving us alone. It was a start, at least.

Leilani sat down on the full cushions with me, letting out a surprised 'oomph' as we both sank far into its velvety depths.

"Thanks for trying," I continued. "Did you want to come out and help the rescue efforts? I need to find Shava."

Leilani ducked her head. "I don't have the stomach for that sort of thing. Lots of people are hurt. I'm enjoying helping care for them once they're here, but I ... um ..." she trailed off, looking lost.

I grasped her shoulders in my hands. Something was clearly troubling her, and we'd been through too much together for me to simply let it go.

"Leilani. What's wrong?"

She tried to keep her eyes on the ground, but her lip quivered and after a few moments she burst into tears, falling against me.

"I'm a horrible person! When the dome fell Duncan tripped and I lost him. I heard him calling my name, but I-I pretended I couldn't hear him! I kept going, and later, when we went back, he was ... he was ..."

I had a few guesses what he looked like, especially if there had been a stampede for safety when the dome had fallen. I wrapped my friend tightly in my arms, holding her close to me.

"Leilani, listen to me. You didn't kill him."

"Yes I did!" she wailed, sobbing into my chest. "I should have gone back. I was his fiancé; it was my job to look after him! I'm a monster!"

I shook her gently. "He was a cursed Noble whose only job was to try to impregnate you before turning into a demon and dying to dragon fire. There was nothing you could have done for him."

She froze at that, shocked. Good. I was trying to shock her.

"But ... but ..." She sniffed. "If he was alive now, the curse would have broken, and he'd be normal!"

I tried to piece together what few flashes I'd seen of her and her betrothed from the ball that night, before everything had gone to hell.

Leilani had paused at the table in front of me, worry in her eyes. Her white dress was stiff and puffy, but suited her light, bubbly personality perfectly. Brightly colored embroidered flowers dotted the hem and her sleeves, snaking down her chest and around her collar. Wooden shoes on her feet gave her added height.

I almost stepped out of the shadows to greet her, but a man followed behind her, a satisfied smirk on his face. I hesitated, not feeling up to meeting another 'new guy' just yet.

"Well? Where is she?"

His red hair was a beacon in the ballroom, bright orange instead of the usual dark red hue I'd seen on other Nobles and Azalea. His face pinched, and lines crinkled around his eyes. He looked much older than her and me.

Leilani flinched, but smiled brightly. "I'll keep looking; don't worry. She's my best friend! She'll want to see me."

"Find her. That's your job tonight." His hand landed heavily on her shoulders, and she nodded. He turned and disappeared back into the crowd. The moment he was gone, the happy smile vanished, leaving only tired defeat behind.

Leilani closed her eyes and took a deep breath, then spun around to face the crowd, her dazzling smile back in place.

I took a guess that wasn't entirely blind. "And would you have been happy with him, had he been normal?"

Blue eyes met mine, filled with tears. "I'm supposed to be," she whispered desperately.

My heart broke for her. "Oh no, Leilani. That's not it at all. The only one whose happiness matters is you. If you are better off without him, then it's all for the best."

She hiccupped and I hugged her again.

"You don't think I'm awful for what I did?" she whispered again as if terrified someone would hear her confession.

"You're an amazing friend and a strong woman," I reassured her, her blonde hair forming a halo around her face as the sun streamed in from the nearby window. "This city will need you, and your kindness."

Leilani sniffed, wiping her face with her sleeve. "Thanks, Mari. You're happy with your guy, right? Or I guess it's guys, isn't it?"

A dopey smile stretched across my face. "Yeah, you could say that."

She beamed at me.

"Pretty girls." Both of us turned our heads as my mother's eyes cracked open, the smallest trace of a smile on her lips.

Leilani gave my hand a pat and excused herself as I practically flew to my mother's bedside, gently tucking a strand of hair out of her eyes.

"Why am I so tired?" she asked, a yawn revealing a

mostly toothless mouth. When had that happened? Or had I simply never noticed?

I gave her a tight smile and patted her hand. "You've worked very hard your whole life. It's understandable you'd make up for it now."

She peeked up at me from under her lashes, her eyes sparkling just for a moment before they closed.

"Get some rest," I whispered into her ear, tucking the covers around her frail body.

My mother fell into a deep sleep, so I ventured back outside. The black dragon was reluctantly put to work, ferrying refugees and other wounded up to the top of the Seat so that Freesia's team could get them settled with new quarters. I spied the queen lying in the shade nearby, being tended to by no less than three people. It was likely the black dragon's price to help. I really needed to find out his name.

Can you take me down on your next trip? I thought at him, causing him to jerk around quickly. A Fireguard carrying a bundle of clothing swore and ducked as the dragon's spiked tail missed his head by inches. The large dragon either didn't notice the near miss, or just ignored it.

The drakling mate. You want a ride down?

And some information about your entire life, I added privately, but the black dragon didn't seem like someone who easily gave away any kind of personal information.

"Yes, please. If it isn't too much trouble."

The black dragon huffed, then took a moment to

swivel his head over in the direction of the queen. The three women around her—primas, if their tattered purple robes were anything to go by—flinched at the dragon's murderous gaze and bumped into each other in their haste to fluff her pillows and wave a fan over her face. Even unconscious, the former queen still had people fluttering around her, catering to her every whim.

I was going back down anyway. It is no burden.

The dragon sidled up next to me, but didn't bend his neck down like Zion and Zariah usually did. His tail whipped out and snagged me around the waist, and dropped me in front of his wing joints before I could even squeak in protest.

'*Hang on!*' was the only warning I got before he ran and jumped off the edge of the Seat. He didn't have neck spikes like Zariah and Zion, so I was forced to wrap my arms around his thick neck and hang on for dear life.

I preferred neck spikes.

My stomach lurched as he sharply dived, then flared his wings as we glided over most of the kingdom. It looked awful, but everywhere I spied devastation, there was also compassion and people helping each other regardless of quarter or class.

Too bad it takes emergencies to bring out the best in people. In the distance, I spotted Zariah, methodically moving large chunks of debris while being directed by a group of a dozen or so people.

How is your ... mate? I asked, attempting to be polite.

The dragon huffed. **Do not pretend to care.**

Well, all right then. I tried again. **What's your**

name? What can you tell us about curses? Were you cursed? We don't know anything about dragons. We—

He cut off my tirade as we neared the edge of the city, landing with much more grace on the hard ground than Zariah or Zion ever had. His tail lifted me up and placed me on the ground.

Too many questions. I don't know how your mates deal with it. Perhaps that is why you have two.

I bit back the snort that threatened to burst from my lips. "Just wait until your mate wakes up," I informed him wryly, smirking. Boy, was he in for it.

He harrumphed, shifting his massive weight from side to side.

Ask one question, then.

My jaw dropped. Just one?! How was I possibly supposed to choose? This was important information about my princes! He couldn't hold it ransom like that! It wasn't fair, it—

I clamped down on my frustration, trying to control myself as he watched me carefully, one giant ridge above his left eye raised at me.

"Fine." I sighed. "What's your name?"

His fangs flashed at me, which I supposed was the dragon way of smiling.

Sabrathan.

I nodded. "Thank you, Sabrathan. For everything."

Sabrathan grumbled, turning to shuffle off to his next crowd of people. **Once my use here is done, my mate and I will leave. We will not say goodbye.**

Abrupt, but that was his choice.

Wind swept through the air, scattering the piles of

ashes and bones that lay scattered everywhere in the ground. They were as numerous as the dusty desert sand. I squinted mine eyes shut to keep the grit out.

"OK," I whispered.

By the time I opened my eyes, he was gone.

CHAPTER
FIFTEEN

I was at the edge of what remained of the mud quarter, which was nothing but ashes. The only reason I knew it used to be my home was because it was the only quarter completely obliterated, thanks to the queen's dragon form.

Sabrathan couldn't take her away fast enough.

With both of my princes busy and my mother sleeping, now was the perfect time to try and find Shava. I couldn't explain why I felt she was here near the mud quarter, where it all began, but it felt right.

I wandered through the ash-covered streets. Small, dirty little mounds were the only evidence of where our huddled homes had been. The alleyways were charred and black. I looked away from the piles of bones and obvious lumps that littered the ground here and there. I walked until I came upon a vicious slant in the ground.

The mine tunnels.

I only made it a few feet toward the tunnel before I

stopped. My hands shot to my face and some sort of gasping noise left me.

Shava.

I'd found Shava.

Her body was twisted and broken as if her attacker had caught her unawares, then had simply dropped her and let her lay after she was dead. With limbs splayed and her head pointed up toward the sky, I forced myself to bear witness to everything.

Including the two holes in her head where her eyes had been.

Including the ruin of her mouth, which pooled with dried, black blood.

Including the hole in her chest, open to her heart and exposing the white of her ribs. Well, where her heart had been.

Someone had taken it.

Unable to stand it any longer, I backed away and threw up. Or tried to. I couldn't remember the last time I'd eaten, so all I managed to do was retch up bile.

What had happened? Who would commit such an atrocity? It was one thing to kill someone, but to ... butcher them? What was the point?

I couldn't leave her like that. I couldn't leave Ell. I'd bury Shava first, then my father.

Then I'd find my boys and demand a hug.

I glanced around the ruined quarter hopelessly, hoping to find a tool of some kind to use. I'd use my bare hands if I had to, but it would take much, much longer to lay Shava to rest that way.

Zariah? Can you hear me?

I hated asking for help, but Shava deserved a quick

burial, and not to rot out here like a piece of carrion picked over by the crows.

Mari. Is everything all right?

I wanted to tell him yes, but it wasn't all right, was it? Instead of anything intelligible I sent a wave of misery down our bond. In turn, his alarm and worry rippled back at me.

Stay where you are. I'm coming!

Gods, I was such a mess.

Soon enough, my hair was buffeted by the shadow of large wings overhead. Zion landed next to me and shifted quickly. Dully, I thought we'd have to figure something out about them shifting and being naked. Could you do anything about that? Learning how to shift with pants would be really useful ...

"Mari? What's wrong? I—"

Zariah stiffened when he came upon Shava, turning around immediately and dragging me with him.

"Never mind, I see." He took a deep breath. "Do you want me to take care of it?" he said in a softer tone.

My head shook back and forth furiously. "No, she's my friend. I need to do it. I just ... I can't ..." I held out my hands helplessly.

"I can help you dig a hole. Would that help?"

I sniffed and nodded, rubbing my eyes. I was crying again. You'd think I'd be all out of tears by now.

Zariah climbed out of the tunnel's entrance and shifted, walking away. The sounds of claws scraping and dirt flying spurred me into movement. I took a breath, holding it as I summoned my courage and grasped Shava underneath her armpits and pulled.

A chattering sound had me stop in my tracks and

crane my head behind my neck to stare back at the dark depths of the tunnel.

What was that?

I waited a few long moments, but my burning lungs forced me to turn away. I dragged Shava up the steep slope, and up onto the flat, ash-covered ground. Zariah turned his large snout as I emerged, already sunk five feet down into his hole.

Good? he asked.

I nodded and he backed out, remaining a respectful distance away. Breathing out through my mouth, I took another breath in while refusing to smell anything. It felt utterly wrong, but I rolled Shava into the pit, wincing as her body hit the bottom with an obscene thud.

I breathed out, gasping and choking. Whether it was from emotion or my gag reflex, what did it matter? Shava and I hadn't been on good terms the last time I saw her, and now I'd never get a chance to fix things with her.

Just another small agony on my long list of trials.

Another odd sound caught my ear. Zariah's dragon head tilted to one side, indicating he'd heard it as well.

Probably just more rocks shifting from the collapse.

"I need to get Ell. Can you take me to him?"

Please, allow me to bring him to you. You can still bury him on your own with your other friend, if that is your wish.

I nodded and sat down roughly on the ground as Zariah took off into the sky. The rumbling and strange sounds continued from the tunnel, an intrusive distraction that kept me from my morbid thoughts.

Zariah's quick return kept me from investigating.

Ell's body was carefully grasped in his bottom claws. Gently, Zariah laid Ell to rest in the same pit as Shava, then backed away. With my bare hands, I began pushing the piles of loose dirt over them, my mind flooding with memories of the both of them.

There was that time a man had been chasing me down an alleyway, and Shava had broken his nose. He'd never chased me again after that.

If I closed my eyes hard enough, I could still feel Ell's solid chest behind me as he drove the chariot, keeping me close and safe as we dashed across the desert.

Neither of them would do anything ever again, and in the end, the brief snatches of time we'd had together would have to do.

I pushed dirt until it stuck under my fingernails, rocks and debris opening red lines on my hands and cracking my skin. Stubbornly, I pushed through until the pain made me pause, falling on my butt to rest and try to shake the sting out of my hands.

Zariah shuffled forward, and made quick work of finishing. He patted the top of the mound a few times with his massive claws, ensuring the dirt was firm and secure.

Without another word, he slit his forearm open with a claw and held it out to me.

I couldn't help that laugh that bubbled forth from me. "A bit of a raw deal, isn't it? One of us always has to be hurting in order to fix the other. Unless that's the point of having three of us?"

Zariah huffed and pushed his bloodied arm at me, impatient.

"No offense, but I want to hurt right now. You

know? Fixing me physically won't fix what's in here." I placed my palm over my heart, pleading with him to understand. "Today, I just want everything to feel how I feel: hurt and broken."

Zariah whined but didn't push me further.

I could tell from his tone that leaving alone in the desert was the last thing he instincts wanted to do, but that fact that he was willing to try if it was what I wanted eased a bit of the pain in my chest.

Was that the strange noise again? Zariah jerked, so at least I knew I wasn't hearing things.

"What is that?" I asked. "I keep hearing it. It sounds close, yet ... not."

The large nostrils on Zariah's snout flared as he swung his head back and forth, trying to scent out the source.

I don't smell anything. It is probably the ground shifting under us where the tunnels collapsed.

Hmm. That made sense. "Yeah. I guess."

I'm going to find Zion. I need to confirm some rumors I've been hearing, and make sure he hasn't passed out from exhaustion yet. Do you wish to remain here for a bit?

"Just for a little," I answered. "Then you can come get me."

Zariah pushed his snout into my neck and nuzzled, then jumped high into the air and pumped his wings. I watched him fly back into the city, passing Sabrathan in the air on his way out. The queen was still unconscious, clutched loosely in his claws.

Goodbye, draklings. Don't die.

I laughed, the first one of mirth I'd had since all of

this had begun. It was good, solid advice from the blunt dragon.

Thank you. Good luck, I called out. Zariah said his goodbyes as well, and I faintly heard Zion. By the faint tone of his voice, he sounded as tired as Zariah had feared.

My stupid, self-sacrificing dragon princes. They made me smile.

My eyes closed as I relished the feel of the sun on my skin, a sensation I'd never known until that fateful day when I'd 'met' the dragon.

"I think you would have liked each other," I said out loud, as if Shava and Ell were next to me, also sunbathing, and not lying in a pit to my left.

"Though Zephyr—" I froze, my brows pinching together. Where *was* Zephyr? Had he been down in the tunnels when they'd collapsed? Perhaps that was for the best; he wouldn't have seen what happened to Shava. Then again, I wouldn't wish death in the tunnel on anyone—dark, crowded, slowly running out of air or bleeding to death, depending on if you were injured when it all fell in or not.

Guilt squirmed in my veins. I was so, so lucky compared to most.

"I know you loved him and all, but he was a dick. Though he didn't deserve to die like that. Nor did you. Or you," I added as an afterthought, thinking of Ell.

I'd never seen a sunset before because the dome had always blocked it. I took my time to watch it now, gazing in awe at the vibrant reds and golds that shifted in the horizon as the sun slowly conceded to the moon and its stars. By the time darkness was just settling over the desert, Zariah returned with Zion on his back.

And food.

"Eat this. Zion says you haven't had anything today."

My eyes rolled at my two nursemaids, but I took the large drumstick and tore off a large chunk of meat, warm juice dripping down my chin. Gods, it was so good. Would I ever get used to the taste of fresh meat? I didn't think it was possible.

I glanced at Zion and shot him an accusing look at the dark circles under his eyes.

"Yeah, I know, I'm one to talk. But I don't feel comfortable resting until we've recovered everyone we could. What if someone was still alive, and me taking a break was the difference between them living and dying?" Honest distress flashed in his eyes.

Zariah huffed. **We've been over this. You can't help anyone if you're unconscious. Sabrathan said—**

"Some help he was!" Zion cut across him, face twisted with frustration. "Lift a few boulders and just disappear with our mother. Wouldn't answer any questions or leave us with any answers. Useless."

I offered him the remaining half of my massive drum stick, one eyebrow raised.

"Zariah made me eat," he grumbled at me, crossing his arms over his chest.

I finished my meal while they stared broodily at the ground.

"Mari, there's something else." Zion's tone was halting, and he shot a look at Zariah as though the golden dragon would stop him at any moment.

I told you that in confidence, Zariah rumbled, getting to his feet and stretching his long body out.

"Mari is our confidence," Zion fired back, which would have warmed me if the news didn't appear to be so dire.

"What is it?" I demanded, tossing my bone to the ground.

"Zariah is trying to dismiss it, but ... we need to leave."

I stared at him, dumbfounded. "Leave?" I asked in disbelief, my voice rising to a higher pitch than I thought possible.

The dragons, at least, Zariah rushed to add. **Those who have been ... organizing things have mentioned that there is a lot of distrust for the dragons. It's understandable. They don't think the kingdom can properly rebuild with us around. There's been too much pain and trauma.**

My jaw dropped. "You saved hundreds!"

"And to many of the people here, another dragon killed thousands," Zion was quick to point out.

My fingers flexed, curling into fists at my side. "I'm not leaving you."

Zion laughed. "We're not suggesting that." He took my hand in his, giving it a squeeze while giving me a pleading look. "Come with us."

Come ... with them? Leave the kingdom?

It was a cruel joke. Some sort of jest. We'd finally defeated the oppressive system that had kept my people down for centuries, and I couldn't stay to see the changes.

"My mother," I whispered pathetically. "My friends."

Zion pulled me into a hug. "I know, flower. I know."

We would never ask you to leave your friends

and family if that wasn't what you wanted, Zariah added, smoke unfurling from his jaw as he gave a sharp look to Zion. Zion let me go, his expression troubled.

I backed away as if physical space from them would give me mental space as well. Could I leave everything behind that I'd ever known? I'd just managed to see things—well, not necessarily set right, but everything was at least changing. It was what I'd wanted to see for so long. It was what the king had claimed couldn't be done.

The king.

"Is your father—"

"The Nobles are in much disarray, but they're united in their support for our father," Zion said. "Zariah, why don't you continue? You're the one who talked to everyone."

The golden dragon shifted, and both of my princes stood before me, tired and disheveled. Their fancy tunics were gone, baring their muscled chests which looked a little thinner than I remembered. The ghost of dark rings were visible under their eyes, which were large and tired. Dirt and ash smeared them head to toe in random places. I wanted to take a rag and wipe every inch of them clean, but it would erase the physical proof of their love for their people and kingdom. The refugees needed to see it.

So it would stay.

Thin, ragged breeches clung tightly to their thighs and bottoms.

"You figured out pants?" I asked, raising one eyebrow.

Zion blushed, and Zariah grinned. "They have to be

extremely tight to shift with us; almost like a second skin."

Huh. At least that would be a handy skill when they had to shift in front of others.

"The curse was broken on the Nobles when you defeated our mother, Mari," Zion began. "The primas and the wives of the Nobles reported that all the afflicted who hadn't yet completed the shift into demons shed all of their ashy skin and were completely cured. There will never be a reaping again, though I suggested every child be brought up to the Seat to learn if he or she wishes it. This is something our father will ensure is carried out."

My throat tightened. "I ... I see."

The king would finally be able to make the changes he'd foreseen all those years ago when he'd married the queen. No longer a stud horse, he would work to ensure things were the way they should be. And the people would trust him, as a former mud boy.

My friends would recover, no longer having to deal with demons for husbands. It was a win-win.

"I ... I just ..."

"It's ok. We understand this is your home." Zion's voice was steady, but his face twitched with emotion. Zariah flat out looked devastated.

Tears leaked down my face. When have I ever cried this much? It had started in the tunnels, and it felt like I hadn't stopped since. "I won't—"

"You do what she wants," Zion grit over his brother, his eyes flashing gold for a brief moment.

And for the first time that I'd ever seen, Zariah backed down to his twin brother.

"Stop being ridiculous. Of course I'm coming with

you. I think. I'm pretty sure." I paused, my heart hurting. "Can I ...? I need to talk to my mother first."

The hope that flared in their eyes hurt almost as much as the thought of leaving my mother and my friends behind.

Zariah took my hand in his. "Of course you can visit your mother, flower. Let's go."

CHAPTER
SIXTEEN

My brother wasn't standing guard outside my mother's room this time, which I took as a positive sign. Zion pushed open the door without bothering to knock.

"Hey! Who—Oh. It's you." My brother stood from where he'd been clearly dozing on a chair, his robes askew and his voice already grating on my nerves. "She isn't up for any visitors. Even the royal ones."

Zion's eyes narrowed, and Zariah's grip on my hand tightened. "Mari has come to say goodbye."

"She isn't—"

Zion and Zariah pushed past my brother's efforts and wrenched open the large oak doors that must have led to the main bedroom. A blonde head gasped and whirled around when we entered, and I dully registered it was Leilani. My eyes, however, were stuck on the emaciated figure lying in bed.

"Mom!"

I pushed Zariah's arms away and ran to her side,

uncaring as I nearly knocked Leilani over in the process.

"What's wrong with her? What's happened? Why didn't you tell me?"

My hands fluttered uselessly over my mother, unsure where I could even touch her. Her hair had turned nearly white since I'd last seen her, and she's gotten so much thinner. Hadn't anyone been feeding her here?

"I wanted to tell you. I wanted to leave to find you, but I also didn't want to leave her alone with him...." Leilani's voice wobbled. Zariah helped her off the ground, and she brushed her dress off with efficient strokes.

I took a few deep breaths. I wasn't angry at Leilani. In fact, I wasn't angry at all. I was terrified.

"Freesia told me you had taken charge of her!" I stomped over to Ess and put a finger in his chest. He winced in pain, and jerked away.

"There wasn't much left to take care of!" he protested. "She was like this when I got here! This girl took over anyway and made me stay out here. It isn't my fault!"

Leilani stood, radiating indignation. "You weren't changing her! She was getting bedsores! Haven't you ever cared for anyone sick before?"

I blinked at the change that had come over my friend. I'd never seen her this impassioned about anything before in my entire life.

"No! Of course not! When someone in the Seat got sick, they were sent to the infirmary!" Ess shouted back.

"Stop it," I hissed at them through my teeth, not wanting to disturb my mother.

Her eyes flickered open, and we all went silent. Too late.

"Mari?"

Her voice was weak, and barely above a whisper. I flew to her side, entwining her bony, thin fingers with mine. She was ice cold.

"I'm here. I'm sorry it took me so long."

A smile twisted her face, the expression so foreign to me it took a moment for me to recognize it for what it was.

"You were busy. Saving the world," she whispered back, drawing up all her strength to pat my hand.

Guilt pushed through me. She didn't know about Ell. She didn't know about Ess being the queen's bed warmer. And she likely didn't know the entire mud district lay in ashes, and a good chunk of the kingdom along with it.

"There are definitely a few changes," I managed.

Ess snorted behind me, and I heard a sound that might have been one of my boys choking back a laugh. He'd snuck up on me.

My mother put her hand out, reaching for Ess. "My boy."

He reluctantly shuffled over, deeply uncomfortable. She grabbed his hand and put it with mine, so all three of us held hands.

"My family. Finally together again." Another dopey smile stretched her face, but of course he started to open his stupid mouth.

Smiling widely, I stomped on his foot under the bed as hard as I could.

Ess made a garbled sound of pain but shut his mouth. He wouldn't say anything to ruin this moment, just like I wouldn't say anything to ruin this moment. Together, we could be united in at least this. One moment where we let my mother have her perfect little family, finally knitted whole.

She didn't need to know about Ell.

"Where is the yellow flower? She's so nice. Everyone has been so nice."

I smiled at that. "Leilani? She is around. It's all right, Mom. I'm glad you've enjoyed it here. I ... might need to leave soon."

Her gaze had been far away this entire time, but for just a moment, it sharpened on me. "Truly?"

I almost took a half-step backwards, but managed to stand my ground. I couldn't remember the last time my mother had looked at me with such recognition and clarity. Ess turned to stare at me, shock in his features.

"Yes," I whispered back. "I met someone. Two someones, really. They can't stay here, so I think I'll go with them."

Her eyes widened with wonder. "Away from here?" she asked, her voice hushed to match my tone.

I nodded because speaking any more would just lead to more tears. I didn't want Mom to see them. Not now.

She cracked first, one large tear escaping from her left eye. "Oh. That's wonderful. It's always been my dream to leave, and here you are, off to see the world. You have a choice. Take it. I'm not sorry."

She yawned, her grip on my hand loosening and her eyes fixating on something far beyond me.

"Sorry for what?" I asked, bewildered. I hadn't heard her talk this sanely in years.

"You were so sick that year you were meant to be reaped. I knew they'd take everyone. Ell told me ahead of time before they came. So I made you sicker. And it worked. They let you stay, and we got more years. You only left when you were meant to."

I stared, all the pieces clicking together. "When I was sixteen and almost died … you did that on purpose?" My voice went unnaturally high.

"Love you," she murmured and drifted back off to sleep.

"Damn," commented Ess behind me. I shook off my shock (and the urge to stomp on his foot again), and gawked at this amazingly strong, brilliant woman in front of me. Ell's comments about her being fearsome were starting to make sense. Just because I hadn't seen it before didn't mean it wasn't there.

Not wanting to wake her again, I carefully detached my hand, and backed away. My shoulders shook as I fought to keep everything reined in. Leilani rushed to my mother's side, touching her neck lightly and putting a palm to her lips.

"She's stopped breathing!" she called out, alarmed. "I—oh. Oh no."

I lost the grip I had on my control. Water dripped onto my arms

It was me. I was crying.

Zariah's arms came around me as my entire world crashed down. My mother had been my everything: my reason to endure. My reason to stay.

I still had reasons to fight: the others in the mud quarters, the little girls, my friends … but those reasons felt dulled. Less urgent. My mother had been my purpose since I was a little girl. Now that she was gone, there was an emptiness that lingered, like a hole in your gum after a tooth had been punched out.

Zion embraced me from behind, and the warm cocoon of my boys slowly filled the torn hole in my heart from my mother's death.

"You made her so happy. She was very proud of you," Zariah whispered into my ear while running his fingers through my hair. "It's OK. Just cry. Do you want us to take care of her for you?"

I knew they were just as exhausted as I was, but I nodded anyway. I was so, so tired, and they had offered.

"I ... I'm sorry. I tried. Even if you don't believe me." Ess's throat bobbed with emotion. At that moment, I realized I didn't hate him. I wasn't even mad at him. I was just tired.

"I know," I said instead, and to my shock, he reached down and gave me a brief (albeit awkward) hug.

"Here, let's get you settled in a bed next door. I'll have some meat and cheese brought up, and we will take care of everything," Zariah interrupted, gently separating us.

Ess's eyes were wide as he watched Zariah pick me up in his arms.

My eyes were already growing heavy as they carried me down the hall and to a different suite of rooms. All of that sounded agreeable. And then, when my mother was laid to rest, we would leave.

Forever.

My eyes cracked open slightly as my body met soft

silk and pillows. Whoever laid me down moved away, and I reached out blindly, not wanting to be alone. I was tired of being strong all the time. I wanted to cry and be held.

Zariah leaned into me, his nose nuzzling my neck as he inhaled my scent. "Mari. You need to rest," he said gently.

My nails dug into the skin of his bare shoulder. He was shirtless; had he just been out as a dragon, then? Memories of how Zion's body had erupted into gold scales flooded my vision, as well as how *full* I'd felt as his cock had shifted and lengthened inside me—

"I need you. Now." I pulled him back down onto me and he wasn't ready, crashing both of us back to the bed with a muffled 'oomph.' My hand slid down his chest to cup his already half-hard cock.

"Not fair, flower," he growled at me.

I was done with the fair. The world wasn't fair, so why should I be? Just when we'd won the day and I had a chance to finally knit my life back together, my mother and my father were stolen from me. I was done caring what others wanted or expected from me.

"Fuck me, dragon boy," I snarled back, daring him to snap.

His hand darted out and snatched my hair, pulling hard as he wound it tightly around his wrist. The burn in my scalp was liquid pleasure in my veins.

"You're only doing this because you're in pain. You want a distraction. Calm down, and we can come back to this when you're in a better frame of mind."

Talk, talk, talk. Good thing I knew the one thing that would set him off.

I wrenched my head to the side and made defiant

eye contact with him, grinning like a possessed woman.

"Make me."

There was a moment of shocked silence where his eyes widened, his pupils dilated, and his nostrils flared. Suddenly, I was flipped around with my face shoved into the sheets, and I was barely able to breathe. He yanked my arms behind my back with a bruising grip around my wrists as he pinned them down against my lower back with one hand. A moment later, his heated body covered mine, his fangs grazing against my ear. I knew I was close when I felt smooth skin give way to prickling scales against my flesh.

"What did you say?" he growled into my ear.

I couldn't help it. He was trying to be so big and scary when I wanted him to destroy me.

I laughed.

My hips lifted from the bed then Zariah was inside me, thrusting into me so suddenly that I gasped and moaned. Hardened ridges stroked in and out of me. Those definitely had not been there before.

"Oh, no. You wanted the dragon, so now you'll take the dragon like a good girl."

Another throaty groan was the only answer I could come up with. I tried to arch my back up against him, but Zariah knocked me back down to the mattress.

He made a choked sound and I felt him swell further inside of me, stretching me to the brink. With a jolt of clarity, I realized how dangerous this could be for both of us. I went still, allowing him a moment to collect himself and regain control. Behind me, all I heard was him gasping for air.

I turned my head to the side, greeted with the most glorious sight I'd ever seen.

Zariah was paused halfway between a shift, his skin gold with scales glowing. Smaller versions of his wings hung from his back, and black claws cut into my skin where he held me down.

He was beautiful.

"Don't ... look ..." he choked out, obviously embarrassed at his lack of control.

I went docile under him, turning onto my back as he released me. I reached out to him, wanting to feel his warm scales rub against my skin.

"Please," I begged him, my eyes stuck to his ridged, scaled cock. It was slightly bigger in this transitional form, and at least this way he wouldn't split me in half!

"Zion will want—"

"Already here."

He both flinched as Zion emerged from the corner, eyes wide and a smug grin on his face. "I smelled you from a half mile away." His eyes raked up and down his brother's partially transformed form. "Neat."

Zion closed his eyes and I watched with fascination as gold scales rippled across his skin, and wings shot out from his back. His face scrunched up in pain and obvious struggle.

"Does it hurt?" I asked gently.

Zariah rested his head against my chest. "No. It is simply ... difficult."

Zion came to the side of the bed and I wiggled my hips until my head was on the edge. I opened my mouth and he grinned, sticking his cock between my lips. I dragged my tongue over the tip and he shuddered, choking when I took him into my mouth in one drag.

"Are you getting off on this, or are you gonna fuck her?" Zion gasped out to Zariah.

Zariah shook his head and lifted my hips, settling in between them.

"I guess you get both dragons, flower."

I didn't even care how loud we were as they made me scream again and again. I screamed until my voice gave out and my leg muscles trembled with exhaustion. I was barely conscious as they carried me to the tub and bathed me, forced me to drink, and put me to bed.

I barely noticed Zariah's kiss at my temple before I was out.

I was warm when I woke up, but that was the only good part. Memories of yesterday flooded back to me, a sob leaving my throat as I remembered my mother had passed. Should I bury her next to Shava and Ell?

Sitting up, I winced at the soreness in my arms and legs from yesterday's exertions. Zion or Zariah would at least help me bury her, if needed. I—

"Mari? Here, have something to eat." Leilani gently opened the door and pointed to a low table, where meat and cheese was set up in a decorative pile on a plate.

"Leilani! My mother—"

"Zion and Zariah took care of it last night after you fell asleep. Is that all right?" she asked cautiously. The strain was evident as I took in the dark bags under her eyes. Leilani was so busy taking care of other people, when was the last time she had rested?

My shoulders drooped. I had given them permission last night, after all.

"Come and sit with me. Let's eat together."

A small smile twitched at the corner of her mouth as she sank gratefully into the cushion next to me with a groan. We grabbed at the meat and cheese together, stuffing our faces and taking comfort in the companionable silence.

After a while, Leilani wiped the crumbs from her mouth with her hand. "So ... you're leaving then, aren't you?" Her eyes were sad even as she tried to smile.

I glanced at the table. "Yeah. Too much has happened here, I guess. And the boys think having dragons around will hurt. At least the refugees get to stay now. We were ready to travel across the desert." I gave a huff at what had been our half-baked plan. Many of them likely would have died in the crossing. Being able to stay was better for everyone.

Just not for me.

"You'll be able to choose your own husband now," I started. "Or none at all," I quickly corrected at seeing the look on her face.

Leilani rubbed her forehead. "I looked for the others, you know. Heather and Hyacinth, Wisteria and Oleria. I can't find them."

I didn't want to hurt her anymore, so I kept quiet about Wisteria and Oleria. "I'm guessing there's a lot of people unaccounted for in the rubble," I offered lamely.

Leilani sighed. "It will take a long time to sort out." Her eyes flared with hope as she tilted her head at me.

"The king is giving an address today. Are you going to go?"

It was tempting. Part of me wanted to have one last talk with the king I'd so briefly bonded with, but it wasn't wise. It would likely be the best time for my boys and I to leave, when the entire kingdom's attention was somewhere else.

"Ah," Leilani said wisely, answering her own question. "Probably for the best."

Silence surrounded us again.

"Freesia is doing so well. She's getting along really well with the king. They're both hard workers," Leilani blurted out, interrupting the quiet.

"Yeah, I bet. Good for her, I guess," I muttered. "She'd be a good queen. Just like she always wanted."

I thought there would be an air of depression and terror that lingered around the kingdom. Countless people were still dead under the rubble, despite the constant clean-up work. And yet, the overall mood was ... determined. Not festive or rambunctious, but full of hope and purpose. It was surreal to see my dream of watching men and women from the mud quarter work side by side with those from the stone, bread, and art quarters, and even Nobles. It didn't quite seem real, and left me feeling adrift and with no real sense of purpose any longer.

They didn't need anyone to save them. They were saving themselves.

I should have been happy. I should have felt relieved.

Instead, I just felt empty.

My entire life, someone had always relied on me. My mother, then the other girls, then the entire mud quarter and everyone in the kingdom. And now?

"Mari! There you are. The king wants to have a word before leaving. Are you ready?"

Zariah stopped his work on the wooden outline of a new house with an eclectic group of people, wiping his hands as he walked over to me. His eyes lit up upon seeing me.

A warm glow ignited in my chest. My boys needed me. And I needed them.

I reached out my arms and he drew me in tightly, tucking my head under his chin. His heartbeat was firm and steady, and just what I'd needed.

"I'm ready when you are. Is Zion coming?" I asked.

Zariah wiped a smudge of ash from my cheek with his thumb. "Already there, flower. Come on."

The streets were chaotic and unrecognizable in the aftermath of the dome's collapse. The only constant that remained and gave me any sense of grounding was the large, raised cliff of the Seat, and the castle. Without those two, I wouldn't have any idea what quarter's remnants I was standing in.

Zariah weaved through piles of debris and groups of people building and baking, collecting and sorting.

"We aren't going up on the Seat?" I asked in confusion. Surely the king would want to give his address up there, wouldn't he?

Zariah didn't answer, but tugged me toward the most recognizable quarter in the kingdom despite its complete annihilation. It was the only one turned completely to singed stones and ashes, after all.

The mud quarter.

Rough houses—actual houses—were in various stages of completion all around me. Instead of being set up in the cramped row we'd lived in before, they made a semi-circle around the edges of the quarter, leaving the middle rows as wide, open spaces. A large platform was almost complete in the middle.

"The king is overseeing the reconstruction of his home quarter personally," Zariah informed me, pride in his voice. "The platform can be used for anything, you see? And around it will be an open market. Everything will be bright and lit, and beyond the market will be the public gardens. The houses you can see on the outskirts. He plans to build them large and airy."

It was hard to suck air into my lungs while my throat was so tight with emotion. I fisted my hand in Zariah's tunic, my knees weakening.

"Mari? Are you—"

"He gets to actually do it," I whispered, more to myself than Zariah. "He gets to actually fucking do what he always wanted."

Zariah softened. "Yeah. He does."

The king was a man transformed up on the raised platform. He stood with Zion and three Fireguards as they bent over a large set of blueprints. Zion's nostrils flared as Zariah and I neared, and he turned around with a large grin on her face.

"There she is! Conqueror of dragons!"

I blushed madly. The king turned and raised one dark eyebrow as Zariah led me up the short steps to see everything for myself, dismissing the Fireguards who continued their conversation without him.

He opened his mouth, but Zion cut him off. "Not

one word about her staying and us ruling. We won't have it. We're leaving before nightfall."

The king's lips pursed into a single line. "It is cruel indeed that when fate finally hands you the tools to your dreams, it also snatches away half of it." His eyes flickered with emotion as Zariah and Zion proudly stood side by side, me in between them.

"I do not care who rules," the king continued. "I want to finally spend time with my sons and get to raise my grandchildren."

My jaw hit the floor even as Zariah's arms squeezed my shoulders. Zion gave a wistful smile, but he didn't back down.

"You know how the Nobles feel. You know how traumatized the people are. We refuse to hide anymore. And if one day Mari wants children—which is completely her choice—what do we do if they're like us? I won't have my child hidden away and thrashed like we were."

Cold horror seeped through me at Zion's implication, and Zariah's tightening grip on me only confirmed it.

The king bent his head. "I'm sorry. I can't change what happened. I—"

"We don't blame you," Zariah emphatically stated, cutting off his father. "We never have. It was no one's fault but mother's; we're just telling you how it is. I'm sorry it can't be different. The people here need a king and stability. Feel free to marry and give them another prince or even a princess to gush over. One without dragon blood in their veins."

An image of Freesia wearing the queen's crown flashed through my head. In it, she held up a swaddled newborn as the crowds cheered her on. It would be poetic and perfect.

It just couldn't involve us.

The king huffed. "Women have caused much grief in my life." He eyed me again. "Though I admit the circumstances were difficult. We shall see."

Zariah smirked. "All I'm saying is we won't begrudge you your happiness, just as you don't begrudge ours."

Zion rolled his eyes. "And who is to say we can never visit? Or write? This isn't goodbye."

Longing crossed the king's face, twisting his features as he fought to keep his stoic expression. "Very well, then," he said gruffly, stepping toward his sons. "Until we meet again."

Zariah went first, letting go of me and seizing his father in a massive hug, wrapping his arms around the old king and squeezing as hard as he could. Silent, unshed tears leaked at the corners of their eyes as they rocked back and forth with each other. With a loud sniff they drew apart.

Zion was slightly more sedate as he hugged the king, but his fingers dug into his father's back so hard his knuckles went white.

"We will visit and find a way to write. You'll be sick of hearing my advice," Zion choked out.

The king huffed. "Just like when you were seven and trying to tell the advisors what to do. Always full of advice."

With a final slap on the back, they separated.

The king turned to me, and my heart skipped a beat with anxiety. I knew I wasn't solely responsible for the princes leaving, but it still felt like I was partially to blame. I took a small shuffle step toward the king, who only tsked at my skittishness and hugged me, picking me up and twirling me around.

"I owe you the most. All those dreams we talked about ... I can't believe the time has come," he whispered into my ear. Before I could respond, he continued with more urgency, "Try to find out more about Hoveria, our birthplace. I will be busy here for quite some time, and in the large mess of things I don't want to waste any scholars on it. It's too personal."

I nodded, understanding.

"I want to learn more about where we came from, if our land still exists, and pass the heritage onto those of Hoverian descent. If you happen to learn anything on your travels, can you send it on?"

It was appalling he even had to ask. "Of course!" I burst out, unable to help it as the tears freely flowed. The king was a good man who wanted to make everything right.

And it would be right. It would be OK.

The king gave my cheek a kiss and broke away.

"Well, we're going to go so we don't linger and make this any more awkward or emotional than it already is," Zariah announced. "Make way for the dragon!"

Alarmed, the other Fireguards on the platform didn't bother to use the stairs as they flung themselves off the platform and rolled when they hit the ground.

I tried hard to smother my laughter, and lost.

In moments, Zariah jumped off the platform and shifted, golden scales filling my vision as the king watched from the platform. Seeing their sovereign unalarmed at the massive dragon that just appeared, the people around him stopped screaming and stared in interest.

"Are you going to take turns flying?" I asked Zion as he helped me climb up Zariah's side and grasp onto his neck spikes.

Zion flushed. "My wings are ... not yet healed. The amount of blood likely needed will put all of us out for a while. We want to find a new home and get settled before we try. Zariah will carry us where we need to go."

With a mighty lurch, Zariah leaped into the air, his heavy wings pounding hard on either side of me. We rose into the air as he took a few laps around the kingdom, giving us all one last looking before heading east.

I gazed down at the Seat, waving in the hopes that Leilani or Freesia would see. My heart reached out as we flew over three identical mounds on the outskirts of the kingdom, flowers lovingly strewn on top.

My mother would be happy I was seeing the world, and I'd like to think Ell would be proud, too. I didn't much care what happened to my brother, but Shava's unsolved death still haunted me.

As we flew, I remembered the strange sounds I'd heard coming from the tunnels when I'd discovered Shava's body. But that was insane, wasn't it? All the demons were dead. Weren't they? Just because I hadn't seen the bodies didn't mean it wasn't true. There were many people who had simply disappeared in the chaos and haven't been seen since: Heather, Hyacinth, and Zephyr.

My thoughts reached out toward Zion and Zariah, normal conversation impossible with how hard the wind whipped around us.

Zariah? Zion? Any idea of how many demons there were down in the tunnels?

I wasn't naive enough to think I'd seen all the tunnels and caves and mines; it was more likely that I'd only seen a fraction.

Zariah grumbled. **I don't know. The curse broke and no one has seen any, so not a problem as far as I'm concerned.**

I bit back a retort as Zion had a more reasonable answer.

I'm sure there were some alive, but all the entrances are caved in. Not even our dragons could dig them out. Perhaps it's for the best.

A lot of people had been saying that lately, me included. Was it though?

As the sun set at our backs, I tried to focus forward on the future. In a place where the landscape was lush and green, and there was water as far as the eye could see. I imagined somewhere my dragons and I could live in peace without fear of being hunted down or exposed.

I even thought about what a child between the three of us might look like.

Smiling to myself, I relaxed against Zariah's warm scales and Zion's steady chest behind me.

Perhaps it was all for the best.

CHAPTER
SEVENTEEN

The trip was long, and we took many breaks. We flew over vast portions of desert, the sands so red it looked like liquid fire. Zariah did all the flying, and I worried over him pushing himself too hard. He never quit until he found a place 'suitable enough' for us to rest, a place with food and water. Sometimes that meant he flew straight into the night.

I worried about him.

Zion was healing, but very, very slowly. He refused to take any blood from me or Zariah, claiming he was fine. I agreed that Zariah needed to keep his strength up, but I wasn't doing anything but riding around! Why wouldn't he let me help?

Then, during the second week of travel, we rested in a shady grove of trees in the middle of a forest. Zion and Zariah had declared the area empty of anything other than wildlife.

Which was why when the woman walked straight into our encampment, we were shocked.

Zariah shifted immediately, taking our several trees and our fire as his massive dragon body filled the clearing.

The woman stepped right up to him with no fear, but did give him a grudging look of respect. She was barefoot and wore a green dress, her brown hair long and wild down her back. Brown eyes took in the three of us, her eyebrows so high they practically melded into her hairline.

"Well, I never thought I'd see one of *you* in person. Let alone meet two." She narrowed her eyes on me. "And a half."

"Who are you? What do you want?" Zion asked, putting himself halfway between me and the strange woman. Zariah growled as he towered over us, smoke wafting from his nostrils.

The woman clapped her hands together as though we'd performed some clever trick.

"Ooh, I can't wait to tell the coven. We thought dragon curses were simply bedtime stories meant to frighten the witchlings. This is incredible!"

Her words finally registered.

"Wait, you know about cursed dragons?" I asked in awe. "Please! You must tell us everything! How does the curse work? What happens next? Where do we—"

The woman held up a hand and I paused. With a flick of her wrist vines and roots sprung from the ground, forming a perfect little seat under her. I stared. Zion jerked and Zariah growled again, ready to burn every twitching vine to a crisp if it came anywhere near us.

"Sit. *Sit!*" the woman commanded, gesturing imperiously to us. Vines and leaves shot out of the ground, and in the blank of an eye, enough seats had sprouted out of the ground for everyone.

Warily, I touched the one closest to me, not entirely ruling out thorns or any other nasty surprises, but the seat was soft and spring, like rich moss. I sat, but wasn't going to let up on my questions. "You're a witch then?"

She tossed her hair playfully over her shoulder. "You don't get out much, do you?"

I grinned. "First time. I'm Mari. This is Zion, and the brute is Zariah."

The 'brute' rumbled from behind me, but at least hunkered down on all fours so he could see and hear the woman better.

"Where to begin?" she breathed out softly, mostly to herself. "Right. Well, as I said, dragon curses were thought to be myths. It's powerful magick, but chaotic magick. White magick of the highest order!"

I settled in firmly against Zion's back, his arms coming to rest around me. "In our kingdom, a witch laid a curse on the queen to turn into a dragon because she had enslaved an entire group of people. These two are her sons, and they are also dragons," I explained.

Her head tilted to the side. "And had they also enslaved people?"

Zion flinched, and I rushed to his aid. "They were bound to obey the queen. They did what they could to correct the wrongs." I paused. "There were also demons. The Nobles who had benefited from the slavery were cursed to turn into demons. The women would turn too, but quickly die. Do you know why?"

It was one blistering question that had never truly been answered.

The witch gave me a look like I was a simpleton. "So there can't be more demons, obviously."

Obviously.

The witch frowned. "Back to your dragons. They weren't the original party cursed?"

I glanced up at Zion.

"No," he answered. "Though someone else postulated that the curse was transferred to us through her womb."

The witch nodded and smiled as if everything made sense. At least someone understood it all.

"Yes, curses can be transferred through the womb, even if centered only on her." The witch glanced between the three of us. "She is your mate then? How fortunate!"

Zariah's head lowered and nudged my neck fondly.

"Yes, very lucky," Zion added, squeezing me protectively.

"Ah. All will be well then. The curse will end with you, provided you don't pass on your dragon genes. I don't recommend it; it's difficult for dragons to find their mates. When they don't, they go feral, then the covens are usually conscripted to track them down and kill them. Wouldn't want to meet any of your progeny that way."

I frowned. "Right ... so, how do they not pass on their ... dragoness?"

The witch grinned. "Simple. Stay human when you fuck. Easy."

Both the man and dragon behind me went rigid.

The witch cackled with delight, rocking back and forth on her self-made chair of vines and branches.

"But ... they're not full blooded dragon, are they? They're half?" I asked weakly, still trying to process all of it.

The witch raised an eyebrow. "Intrigued, are you? Well, live your best life. You might be fine. Then again, you might not. Best not to risk it, eh?"

Her eerie gaze snapped to Zion and Zariah, who took half-steps back at her utterings. "Oooh, something exciting will be afoot. When her time comes, you come and get me, you hear? This will be the beginning of something wonderful; I can already tell!"

I wanted to ask more, but the vines and branches snatched out, wrapping around the witch and obscuring her from view. When they finally cleared, the witch was gone.

Zariah huffed, and we eventually moved on after a full night of rest.

CHAPTER
EIGHTEEN

The island was lovely. It was warm, and most importantly, so green I thought that some days it would bleach my eyes. Flowers and birds and insects and life itself thrived everywhere. It was the complete opposite of desolate wasteland that surrounded Barcenea.

Zion and Zariah still felt bad about it. Hopefully in time, the landscape would recover.

In the beginning, when we'd first set out east, they'd asked me over and over again if I wanted to seek out my home land of Hoveria. I didn't need to be here to keep searching. I could do it from anywhere, and perhaps we'd even learn more on our travels.

The past was in the past, and I couldn't change it. Knowing what I missed out on wouldn't change me as a person, it would only bring about more heartache. And I'd already had my fair share.

My future and my life included my boys.

And the large lump growing inside of me.

He's not a lump, argued Zariah immediately, growling from somewhere high, high above me. He was miles away, but we heard each other as clearly as ever. The closer our bond got, the more of each of others' thoughts we could hear. After a lifetime of secrets and surviving, it was freeing to have someone just know every truth that passed through your mind. There were sometimes hurt feelings of course, but the unshakable bond between us had only grown through understanding each other.

I'm growing it. I get to name it. It's a lump, I shot back, refusing to back down on this.

Zion lifted a scaly brow, his eyes cracking open from where he was sunning himself on the beach. Dragons loved the beach. Who knew?

I wiggled my toes deeper into the sand, relishing the coolness the wet earth had to offer.

I—

Whatever I'd been about to say next was cut off by a warning roar from Zariah far off in the distance. Zion had sprung to his feet a hair's breadth before his brother had cried out, both of their dragons sensing immediate danger.

I stood as well, not that it meant anything. I could hardly climb up into our treehouse home as big as I was now, and relied on my boys to carry me everywhere while this child cooked inside of me.

It's the black dragon! warned Zariah. **He's approaching from the south, he'll get there before I can!**

Zion roared, snapping me up in his claws carefully and fleeing from the beach, back deep into the jungle of the island.

Hey! Is it Sabrathan? Put me down!

I beat my fist twice against his claws, our universal sign that I wanted down. For the first time since we'd come here, Zion ignored me. Carefully, he deposited me onto the large bamboo platform in front of our treehouse, then whirled around and darted off into the sky. I couldn't see anything due to the thick canopy of trees.

"GODDAMNIT," I shouted at no one, frustrated beyond belief. I wasn't fucking crippled just because I was pregnant! I eyed the rope ladder next to me that went all the way down to the ground. If I was just careful and took it one rung at a time ...

A dragon roared and screeched, a dragon that wasn't Zariah or Zion.

"Fucking men," I complained to the air and hurried down the ladder as quickly as I dared. Stupid dragon men and their stupid pride. All men were the same in some areas no matter what the species!

Hobbling like a fat little bird, I pushed aside leaves and vegetation as I followed the large path we'd cut through the jungle toward the overlook that would give me a good view of north. The west side of the island had gently sloping beaches, but the east had perilous, rocky cliffs. We'd decided to build our house in the jungle but also on the side of the large mountain that stretched toward the heaven in the middle of the island. The boys said it was defensible; I'd simply liked the view.

A dragon roared in pain. Zion, if I had to guess.

And now, as I scrambled on my hands and knees as fast as I could up the side of the hill to the overlook, it granted me the perfect view as Sabrathan came at me hard, determination and fire in his gaze. I stood and met his eyes squarely, bracing my feet under me and placing my arms protectively around my stomach.

His gaze shifted imperceptibly to my rounded middle, and a somber sound came from his throat. Zariah was behind him, gaining ground fast. Snapping branches and the smell of smoke told me Zion had fallen into the forest and was trying to burn his way through it in order to reach me.

Fucking calm down, I ordered all of them. **I will handle this. Sabrathan is a friend!**

I felt rather heard the raging protests of my two mates, and I snarled in response.

I am your mate, and you will listen! I screamed internally. **I am not injured or helpless! Now STAND DOWN.**

Shocked silence met me through the bond, but Zion belched a stream of fire half a mile wide into the air in frustration. Zariah dove onto the side of the mountain a decent distance away, but high enough that he felt comfortable he could quickly intervene if something happened.

Thank you, I sent back through our bond, knowing this was hard for them. Ceding control to what their dragon viewed as a very tiny, very breakable human girl was something we constantly worked on.

And they were getting better.

So I stood firm as Sabrathan flew straight for me, seemingly on a collision course with me and the top of the hill until he flared his wings hard at the last moment, sending trees and branches and my hair blowing backwards with the force of the gale. My eyes squeezed shut from the sudden wind, so I didn't see what he had clenched in his claws until he set it gently at my feet. Feeling something soft and warm, my eyes shot open.

He gave me blankets. Thicky, heavy blankets that unfurled slightly as they rolled toward me. I bent down toward, flinching and jumping back as the bundle twitched and moved.

"Sabrathan?" I asked warily, my heart pounding.

Sabrathan dug his claws into the side of the cliff and hung there, wings flared. I realized he was waiting ... for me.

Mari ... Zariah whined in my head, Zion sending his frustration along down the bond with it.

Shut it and let me investigate, I snapped at both. I would make it up to them later, since I knew they were only trying to protect me.

Tentatively, I reached a hand out and pulled back the top layer of blanket.

Vivid lavender eyes met mine, and iridescent white scales flashed every color before me, a rainbow of beauty and perfection. Tiny little wings tried to flare and couldn't, bound by the blankets tangled around it. Its little cheeks huffed and puffed, pumping its small fists and legs and getting nowhere. Puffs of black hair floated about her little porcelain features.

"Oh my gods," I whispered.

What is it? Zion asked, unable to help himself. Both him and Zariah inched closer and closer, crawling up the cliff behind me like two large, scaly guardians. Curiously, they peered over my shoulder at the bundle.

Not a dragon—

Nor a human—

"Shut it, both of you," I said in a hushed voice, still

stunned. I reached out and plucked the little humanoid baby with wings and scales from the blankets, holding it in my arms. It was a creature I'd never seen before, half-human, and half-dragon.

Her name is Nuri, Sabrathan breathed out, unable to meet my gaze. **Please, I helped save your mate when he was crushed. I helped your city when it fell. Please ... help ... me ... now.**

The despair in his voice burrowed under my skin and clung there. I knew from experience how hard it was for a dragon to admit defeat and ask from others.

"Sabrathan, where is your mate?" I asked gently, backing up so he had room to comfortably land.

The black dragon crawled up onto the ledge and hunkered down on his belly, ears tucked back against his skull and his head on the ground.

He didn't need to say it; I understood. So did my mates.

We are sorry for your loss, Zariah intoned seriously. Zion made a sound of agreement behind him. They got down on all fours as well, resting their heads on the ground in solidarity with the massive black dragon.

"Nuri is a beautiful name," I said to the baby, smiling as I held her up in the sunlight. Her scales sent a kaleidoscope of color bursting across my chest and face.

It was my fault. I ... My mate was not strong enough to give birth. She would not shift into her dragon form. If I had not lost myself to instincts ... Sabrathan broke off, too despondent to continue as he scraped his snout into the ground. I hugged the baby close to my chest, her struggles ceasing as she put her head next to my heart beat.

"Why are you here?" I asked, though I was confident I already knew what he would ask.

I do not know how to care for a child, he admitted, his voice breaking. **I killed my mate. I do not wish to kill my child. She deserves better. She deserves**—He cut himself off, viciously shaking his head side to side.

I reached a hand out and laid my palm firmly on his massive snout, giving him a physical presence to focus on. Sabrathan went still, calming under my touch.

"She can stay under one condition," I demanded of him.

A whining sound left his throat. **Anything,** he begged.

I smiled, directing my thoughts to everyone. **You stay with us. She deserves to know how much her father loves her, and how much he loved her mother, even if your time was cut short.**

Sabrathan reared back as though I'd asked him to cut his wings off. I turned my attention to the baby, still marveling at the odd, yet beautiful creature in my hands. She stared at me seriously, her little brow crinkling with effort. With a quiet whispering sound, her wings sucked into her back and her fangs retracted. Her scales flashed then disappeared under smooth skin, barely visible to the eye.

I blinked in surprise as I held what now appeared to be a normal human baby, albeit with glimmering skin.

"Eee!" Nuri swiped at my hair and giggled, clearly pleased with herself.

Did ... did you know she could do that? Zion asked, just as taken aback as I was. Zariah stuck his head over my shoulder to gently nuzzle the baby, who gave me an impressive little roar as she laughed and snarled at his dragon's face.

You are the first human she has seen, Sabrathan offered. **When she was born, my mate ... I ... did not want her to see her mother's body. I took care of it quickly.**

I never wanted to hug anything more than the giant mess of a dragon in front of me. Nuri couldn't stop snuggling into me, touching my hair and soft skin, comparing it to her own. I had so many questions, but they weren't appropriate now.

You told me it was impossible in dragon form, Zion pouted privately to Zariah and me.

Zariah hissed and swiped at Zion's head. **Sabrathan *killed* his mate.**

To be fair, the birth killed her. Not ... the act, I interjected.

So he claims, Zariah shot back.

Sabrathan stayed on his belly, watching patiently as we decided his fate, and the fate of his daughter.

Does that mean if they both would have been dragons they would have had a dragon baby?

I closed my eyes, willing my boys to shut up. Now wasn't the time.

Zion shifted back into his human form, hands eagerly held out to hold the baby. I handed her over after a small nod from Sabrathan. Zion's eyes were huge as he took in the tiny baby who held so many of his mother's characteristics.

"I guess this would make her our half-sister,

doesn't it?" he said carefully, a touch of awe in his voice. Zion glanced up at Sabrathan, flashing a winning grin. "That makes you family, you know. You can't go anywhere."

Zariah huffed from us, stubbornly still in dragon form.

I gave Zion a significant glance, arching an eyebrow at him. He rolled his eyes good naturedly, handing the baby back. As he shifted into dragon form and tackled Zariah, I smiled tightly at Sabrathan.

Zariah's roar of frustration echoed over the valley as they both tumbled down the cliff, biting and clawing at each other. With one hand, I patted Nuri on the back, swaying back and forth. Sabrathan's head tilted to the side.

Should I ...

I waved a hand dismissively. "Let them fight. It's good for them to get the piss and vinegar out every now and then. You could always spar with them sometimes. We've found it helps them keep their dragon instincts in check."

Sabrathan flinched as if I'd struck him.

"Oh no, I didn't mean it like that!" I insisted, imploring him to understand. "It's all about practice and having others around to help. You've been alone so long, haven't you? Here, let's start simple. When was the last time you were in your human form?"

He stared blankly at me.

"So the first time I saw you then," I asked weakly, taking this as confirmation about how he'd manage to have a half-human, half-dragon baby.

I ... don't remember. I have simply ... always

been this way. There has been no reason to change. Other than that one time.

It was on the tip of my tongue to ask if it would have been worth it for his mate, but I resisted.

"OK, well, let's try again now," I suggested brightly. Both of us ignored the roars and blasts of heat coming from a half mile away.

Sabrathan hunkered down on all fours. I waited patiently, but absolutely nothing happened.

I can't do this. I don't have a human form, I—

I raised a hand, stopping him. Glancing down at Nuri's little head nestled against my chest, an idea bloomed.

"Focus on Nuri. Focus on the smoothness of her skin, and the clear planes of her back. Look at her round fingers and toes, and focus on how she feels against you."

Sabrathan closed his eyes and took a deep breath. Nothing happened for a long time, but I was patient. So was he.

When something finally did happen, it was so subtle I almost missed it. His wings shrunk ever so slightly.

Nuri squealed, and he cracked one eye open. He stared at her, and the changes came faster. He shrunk inch by inch, wings painstakingly sliding one small bit at a time into his back. His claws and fangs sank away just as slowly, each disappearing scale a victory.

I wasn't sure how long it took, but I dimly registered that the jungle was quiet again, empty of the sound of two warring dragons. Perhaps Zion finally won one over Zariah, but unlikely.

When the transformation was over, the same half-dragon, half-man stood in front of me again, with scales glinting just underneath his skin. Could he not fully shift into a human form because he was out of practice?

I rushed over to offer my free hand to support him, and he gratefully leaned on me. Dark, curly black hair in heavy braids went down to his waist, but his eyes remained a vivid gold.

"Sabrathan?" I asked.

Zariah and Zion dropped from the sky and shifted, landing with precision in a crouch in their human forms. They stood and took in Sabrathan's new form with surprised looks.

"Nuri, this is your father." I gently pushed the baby into his arms, staying close in case his new arrangement of limbs caused him to accidentally drop the baby. I needn't have worried—he took his daughter with all the security in the world, holding her tightly to him. She squawked a bit at being squished, then eagerly grabbed one of his long braids and pulled.

An odd, choked huff forced itself from Sabrathan. His first laugh.

The four of us gathered around the new little life, thoughts swirling about as I rubbed my enlarged stomach.

"Will our child be ... similar?" Zariah asked, unable to help himself.

Sabrathan glanced up, eyeing me with a frown. "Did you take her in dragon form?" he asked point blank.

I blushed like mad while my boys' expressions grew stormy.

"It will be fine," I insisted. "Remember the witch?

She said to call on her when it was time. We could always ask her for help."

I could feel the panic rising in my mates.

"My ... mate was not well," Sabrathan gruffed out, voice rough and gravelly from disuse.

"You see?" I pressed, plastering a big smile on my face. "It will be fine."

Zion frowned, but Zariah moved in closer to have a better look at Nuri. "A half-dragon, half-human baby. Is there a name for such a thing?"

Sabrathan shook his head.

"Let's make one," I insisted brightly.

Sabrathan ran a finger slowly down his daughter's cheek, marveling at the softness.

"I have a word. From a different language far away."

"What's that?" I asked.

He smiled at me, teeth blindingly white. His first smile.

"Draken."

Chapter Nineteen

Despite that all-consuming darkness around him, the demon felt the dragons leave as if they were two large, golden stars drifting further and further away.

Power flowed through his veins, humming maniacally and barely under control. It was a struggle to keep it contained these past few days since the ritual, but now that the dragons were gone, it was time.

With a loud scream he pushed the white magick out through his veins, forcing it into the dead and dying around him—his people! His salvation!

Groans and shrieks and moans warped into a dissonant chorus so loud and thunderous he felt it thrum in his chest and throat.

Rise my brothers and sisters! Rise!

But the sisters did not rise ... only the brothers.

He frowned at this unexpected development. Had he done the ritual wrong? Had it had something to do with the sacrifice he used?

It didn't matter in the end. Not really. Power and magick ripped through his veins like an uncontrollable fire. Wherever he ended up taking his people, they would simply *take* the women they needed. He would continue to experiment and tinker, making himself and his people stronger until they were rulers of the world! Those who shunned and discarded them would feel the cold bite or iron shackles around their necks and wrists!

Everyone would be sorry for forgetting about them. Everyone would be sorry for letting them rot underneath the dark and dirt. They would see the might of magick and the demons would rise—across the desert, over the mountains, and THEY WOULD HAVE VENGEANCE.

It was the only thing that mattered. It was his only purpose.

Summoning his people, he gave a yell and gathered his magick. He *pushed*.

It was good the dragons were gone. If they weren't, they might have been able to see the single hand shoot from the rubble of an old mine tunnel, black with white glowing runes embedded in its skin.

THE STORY CONTINUES...

THE LOST PRINCE
RAVEN STORM

Cast aside since birth and denied my true heritage, they know me as the bastard prince. For years I played their game, doing allI could to assist my half-brothers shuffle refugees from the castle, while keeping them and the dying Nobles safe in the old mine tunnels.

The Prince of Rats, one girl called me.

The others view the curse as their doom, but they don't realize the golden opportunity it presents. With magick coursing through my blood, I've greedily hoarded all the knowledge I could. They left us all for dead, and once I'm through with them, they'll wish they'd stuck around to finish the job.

All of Dorea will tremble under the might of their new Overlord.

Preorder now

Acknowledgments

Thank you to my close friends who put up with reading all the early drafts and sticking with me to see the full story come to fruition. Thank you to my ARC team for pointing out mistakes and errors. Thank you to my husband for putting up with my long hours of intense focus and making sure our children aren't running around feral in the process. Thank you for believing in me and supporting my dreams to write. Thanks to my editor Carrie, who did a fantastic job and couldn't have been more helpful.

Thank you to all the readers who support me. YOU are who I write for. Join my newsletter or reader group below to stay up to date with the latest in releases and contests!
-Raven Storm-

Want to read Raven's rough drafts as she writes them, and give input? Join her REAM today!
https://reamstories.com/writerravenstorm
Follow Raven on all of her social media platforms below
Tiktok: @writerravenstorm
IG: @writerravenstorm
FB: http://www.facebook.com/writerravenstorm

Youtube: www.youtube.com/@writerravenstorm

Newsletter: https://dashboard.mailerlite.com/forms/83943/73668655639955300/share

Reader's Group: www.facebook.com/groups/207690987663684

Also by Raven Storm

Kingdom of Flames & Flowers

Kingdom of Ash & Bones

Rise of the Drakens Series

The Lost Siren

The Lost Alliance

The Lost Kingdom

The Lost Nation

The Lost Princess

The Lost Child

The Lost King

The Lost Prince

Rise of the Alpha Series

Chained: Rise of the Alpha Book 1

Claimed: Rise of the Alpha Book 2

Changed: Rise of the Alpha Book 3

Box Set with Bonus Scenes

Aggie's Boys

The 40-Year-Old Virgin Witch

The Witch Who Couldn't Give Amuck

Hex Appeal

The Demon Chronicles (YA)

Descent

Feud

Royal Hunt

About the Author

Raven Storm is an emerging author of dark fantasy & why-choose romance. She loves to write, has three amazing children, and resides in the northeast with her husband and cat, Arthur. When she isn't writing, Raven is teaching and performing music, or coaching softball.

Printed in Great Britain
by Amazon